Tomorrow Belongs to Me

to Me

Mark Roberts

Andersen Press • London

First published in 2004 by
Andersen Press Limited,
20 Vauxhall Bridge Road, London SW1V 2SA
www.andersenpress.co.uk

British Library Cataloguing in Publication Data available
ISBN 1 84270 304 8

Phototypeset by Intype Libra Ltd
Printed and bound in Great Britain by
Mackays of Chatham Ltd, Chatham, Kent

Tomorrow Belongs to Me

By the same author

Night Riders

The 12-Day Jinx

I'd like to thank:
Conrad Williams for his great humour and constant solidarity.
PC Peter Garrett and the Merseyside Police Force whose help
have made much of this book possible.
My wife Linda without whom very little would be possible.

The author and publishers gratefully acknowledge permission
to reprint lines from 'We'll Meet Again', Words & Music by
Ross Parker & Hughie Charles © Copyright 1939 Dash Music
Company Limited. Used by permission of Music Sales
Limited. All Rights Reserved. International Copyright
Secured.

For Kris, Jack, Beth, Will and Eleanor

Contents

1

Easy Come, Easy Go

For a second or two, I pictured myself sitting on the front row of the multi-screen cinema near home, looking up at a towering image of Me on the wide screen and witnessing the look of horror spreading across my face. Little Me and Big Me, Little Me slumped in the seat, Big Me stretched across the screen. Little Me sinking, second by second, further and faster into the seat, as the blood drained from Big Me's face. And then, as all things must, the moment passed and total reality took over.

The total reality was this. It was four hours since I'd walked out of my mother's house. I'd boarded a National Express coach for London (one way ticket from Liverpool, £12.50). I'd taken with me one Nike sports bag, with as many clothes as I could pack into it, and my building society book (life savings, £250.73). I was well on my way to London, or so I thought, when the driver announced over the loudspeaker that the radiator was overheating and he was pulling into the next service station to get it sorted.

I sprinted to the Gents and pushed open the end door cubicle, dropping my Nike bag on the tiles just outside, all of a sudden desperate to use the toilet.

Unease mushroomed inside me, the sure and certain feeling that something very bad was happening. Something was extremely wrong but my brain refused to get into gear. I looked behind me, across my shoulder, and eyed the collage of race hate graffiti and tribal football slogans that covered the closed door of the cubicle. My bag? Outside the cubicle. I opened the door with the other hand and saw that my bag, in which my whole world was packed, was gone.

Where there'd been twelve silent figures only moments earlier, now there were three. 'Anyone seen anyone leave here with a Nike bag?' They all eyed me and they all ignored the question, just as I'd have done in their shoes. The words echoed round the room like a sound bite from a Science Fiction video. And it was then, at that precise moment, that I saw myself in the cinema near home. Little Me and Big Me. The moment came and there I was, in a public toilet of a motorway service station in the middle of nowhere, robbed of everything I owned save the clothes I stood up in and the contents of their pockets.

I saw myself, in graphic widescreen, sinking deeper into the dirt, stunned and drowning in thin air.

I don't know how I got to the service station restaurant or even why I ended up there. I just walked like a stranger to the planet, taking the alien world one footstep at a time, while my heart pumped at my ribs, It's gone, it's gone, it's gone . . .

I reached into my Levis and found a handful of loose change that amounted to just over £1.50, enough for a cup of tea, a chance to sit down and the room to at least try some straight-thinking.

The walk along the servery was a painful one, spiced with visions of prawn mayonnaise sandwiches and lemon meringue pies, roast chicken and chips and . . . I closed my eyes as the woman ahead of me in the queue took a slice of chocolate fudge sundae and placed it on her tray just beside the plate of bacon and eggs.

Why hadn't I eaten before I left home? Why? I asked myself. I just hadn't been hungry at all at the time. And all the while, my stomach growled, What about me? What about me?

I sat at a table overlooking the car park and motorway and counted out the money I had left, the change from my tea, all 43p of it. How, I wondered, as I sipped my tea, am I going to get by? Then I wondered, as the one and only National Express coach pulled out of the car park, how am I going to get to London? The driver, radiator obviously fixed, was leaving without me. A sour taste overwhelmed the back of my throat, like I was about to be sick, and then faded back as the coach disappeared into the fast moving lines of traffic on the motorway.

★   ★   ★

In my last but one row with Mum (four out of ten for volume and sheer unpleasantness, no shrieking or smashed plates but no love lost either), she'd pointed her finger at me and repeated over and over in the sing-song voice she used when she was dead angry but just about still in control, 'Easy come, easy go! Easy come, easy go!'

It was true, I was always losing things, things like fountain pens, school books, CD cases, and now even everything I owned in the entire world.

'You wouldn't lose your stinking jacket!'

She was right, of course; I took great care of my brown suede jacket. It was my pride and joy and I'd spent six months on the worst paper round in Liverpool to pay for it when Mum had flatly refused to buy it for me. 'You want it, you earn it!'

I was glad that the clothes I stood up in were the best ones I owned. Beneath my suede jacket, I had a black Benetton T-shirt and, between that and my Adidas trainers, a pair of blue Levi 501s that my absentee father had kindly posted to me at Christmas from his love nest in France; which made me think, *What would Dad do in my situation*? I could almost hear Mum's voice in my ear whispering through clenched teeth, 'Do what he always does when the going gets tough, run away! Like father, like son!'

I pressed my face into my hands and wondered if it was all some nightmare, if I'd wake up ice-cold and sweating wildly in the pit of night, when I heard a voice, asking, 'Are you OK?'

I looked up at the sound of a voice, shocked that it came from no further than the other side of my table. I hadn't been aware of anyone coming near me, let alone sitting across the table from me, within touching distance.

The voice, like his presence, seemed to arrive from nowhere. Across the table, his elbows perched on the surface, chin on the back of his hands which were joined together by his criss-crossed fingers.

'You were miles away,' he said, his clear blue eyes not leaving mine. I found myself staring at his eyes, their blueness like a picture book sea, the black pupils at their centre, jet black, like a pair of curled-up and frozen ants. His hair was even darker still and seemed to have traces of blue where the light fell on his head.

I had the feeling I'd seen him before, in a film, or in a rock band, or on the front of a magazine. He had the good looks and assurance of a person on the verge of making it in a big, big way, or to put it another way he had all the good looks and assurance that had been denied me and any number of other so-so looking fifteen-year-old lads.

He leaned forward, very slightly, and I became aware of the soft creaking and vivid scent of a brand new leather jacket. I maintained my silence while I scrambled through the garbage dump inside my head for something to say, something cool or intelligent and bound to impress. At the end of the rummage, I cleared my throat and offered this stunning question.

'Do I know you . . . or what?'

He shook his head, smiled and indicated with his now unlocked hands. 'I was just passing by and I noticed you looked a bit bothered. Well, to tell you the truth, I saw you were crying and wondered, are you OK?'

My fingers flew to my face, my wet and tear-stained face. Without realising, I'd been crying and the tears must've been tripping down my cheeks. I wiped at my face with the backs of my hands. He reached out a hand and offered me a lily-white linen handkerchief which I almost snatched from him; as he gave it to me, he squeezed my arm very briefly and gave me a smile that seemed to say, *Don't worry about a thing!*

'I'm sorry,' I said, wiping my eyes. 'Crying like a baby.'

He shook his head and leaned back in his seat. 'What do you call a man,' he asked, 'who says he doesn't cry?'

'I dunno,' I replied.

'Liar. What do you call his friend who also doesn't cry?' I shook my head and he told me, 'Corpse.' His laughter was warm and infectious and I found myself chuckling along with him even though I didn't like the gag; here was clearly a guy who liked his own jokes a lot. 'Listen,' he said, straightening up. 'Seriously. Is everything all right?'

'Yeah,' I answered without really thinking and then, 'No, not really!'

He reached his hand across the table and shook my hand very firmly, telling me as he did so, 'My name's Luke, Luke Frears.'

'Danny Anderson,' I returned the courtesy and withdrew my hand.

'What's up, Daniel?' *Daniel?* No one called me that.

'I've just left home!'

'Run away?'

'Run away, yeah, and, my bag's been nicked and the bus has gone without me and so all I've got is 43p and the clothes I'm wearing . . .'

'Not a very encouraging start. Still,' he said, as he

turned away and looked at the paradise alley of the food servery. 'Have you eaten?' he asked. I didn't answer. 'Don't go away!' he said, heading off and picking up a tray. I was too hungry and too curious to move a muscle and when he returned a few minutes later, tray laden with hot tea and chocolate fudge sundae, and double portions golden brown chips and deep pan cheese and onion pizza, I was then just too grateful for words.

'Dive in,' he said.

'Thanks.'

I wasn't being rude or greedy when I demolished my meal and half of his but the bottom line was I didn't know where, when or if I'd be eating again.

As I finished spooning chocolate fudge sundae into my overactive mouth, I became aware of his hands and the silver keys he turned between his long tapering fingers, and the way he was smiling at me like he'd known me for years.

'Are you feeling a bit better now?' he asked.

I nodded, mouth full, smiled back, swallowed and replied, 'Yes . . . thanks, much better, thanks very much . . .'

And without a further word, he stood up, turned and walked away.

2

Hunky-Dory on the Big Bad Globe

I followed. I followed Luke, without invitation, to wherever it was he happened to be heading. And now, as we weaved our way past the Volvos and the Fords, the Fiats and Saabs, the prospect was this: he'd go his way and I'd go mine, meaning I'd be back on my own again, my head just above the surface but just waiting for the next stroke of mayhem to send me sinking under.

I wanted to ask for a lift so badly that the words seemed to jam in my throat. I found myself blinking too quickly and staring at the keys as he casually jangled them in the sharp sunlight. I was fascinated by them, like a cat following the toy in its owner's hand and in the width of the world and the scope of the sky, at that moment, nothing else really mattered.

'That's my heap!' he said, pointing, jolting me from the keys' voodoo as sharply as a slap on the back. I took a deep breath of air and I asked,

'Did you say heap or jeep?'

As I admired the black sheen of the bodywork and the curve of the large wheels, my eyes were drawn to the comfort of the seats and the sheer space and luxury of it. It was a brand new Range Rover; and because the *one* issue I ever agreed with my mother over was that it was rude to ask strangers questions about their money,

I was horrified to hear myself saying, 'Where'd you get the money for that then?'

He laughed and replied, 'I got some compensation.' Having already pushed my luck way too far, I strangled the words, '*Compensation, oh what for?*' and watched with growing dread as he eased his way into the driver's seat.

He pointed to the passenger door, so casually, and uttered the magic words, 'It's central locking, Daniel!' In an instant, the world stopped wobbling beneath my feet and the sky stopped pressing down on my skull.

'Thanks,' I blurted, as he slid a CD into the machine and a bone-crunching metal beat growled through the speakers.

As I climbed in, I noticed a camcorder on the seat behind mine with a box of video tapes. He caught me spying, and started explaining, 'I'm making a film, a documentary about whatever catches my eye.'

'Like a video diary?' I said.

He started the engine. I dreamed of making video diaries.

The camcorder looked expensive, as did the suitcases in the luggage space at the back. Everything I could see or touch smelt bright brand new and so I guessed Luke must have been on the smart end of some massive compensation payoff.

And we were on the motorway, drifting into the middle lane, sitting high, close to the cars below, looking down on other people's lives and passing them by.

This is just a dream, this is not a dream . . . The words appeared from nowhere and spun around the outside of my head . . . *not a dream, just a dream* . . . they echoed, next, within the curve of my skull. And were gone.

He turned the volume right down and asked, 'Daniel? Let me guess. You were heading for London, weren't you?'

'That's right,' I replied. 'How'd you guess?' I noticed all the road signs that mentioned London were pointing away from the direction in which we were heading and Oxford seemed to be the biggest town in our direction.

'How'd you know I was going to London?' I asked.

'Oh, call it an educated guess!' He was smiling broadly. 'That's where everyone goes, Daniel, when they're on the hoof from home. That's where they go to make their fortune or wind up dead!'

He turned the music down even further until it was a blur in the background, and shifted into the inside lane, slowing down in equal measure as he did so.

'How do you mean, *dead*?'

'It's a dangerous place when you're homeless and broke.'

'Yeah, but—'

His smile was dissolving into deadpan.

'Yeah, but what?' he asked.

'Yeah, London, that's where I was heading. It's a big place, I'd find work and avoid hassle. I'd be just another face in the crowd.' We hit the tail end of a traffic jam. The sun, bright, cold and blinding, reappeared suddenly from behind a dense bank of cloud.

'What would you do if you woke up, Daniel, and there was some scumbag standing over you with a knife?

What would you do?' *I'd scream and beg for mercy*! I instinctively thought, but somehow this didn't sound like a good enough answer.

'If someone pulled a knife on me?' I was talking fast and thinking on the tips of my toes.

'If someone pulled a knife on you?' he reiterated the question. 'Come on, what would you do?' He had a way of asking the toughest question in the kindest of voices. He turned the CD off. A bridge of silence formed between us.

'I'm fast on my feet, I'd try and get away!' I tried to sound hard but how weak and feeble my words appeared. I tried again. 'Or I'd put up a fight!'

'Fair enough,' he whispered, and looked directly at me. 'But what if there were four of them. You can't fight four armed headcases!'

'Why? Why pull a knife on me? Why would they pull a knife on me?'

He pulled a pair of shades from his shirt pocket and I felt my spine arch with instant fear. Their metal frame caught in the bright sunlight, making them glint suddenly like an unflicked blade. But it was a pair of shades, that was all, not a knife, not a threat. Suddenly, I was feeling on edge of the edge, imagining for a fleeting moment that my fellow traveller was about to slice me open when all he was doing was reaching for his sunglasses. He put them on and immediately looked cool enough to walk through a burning oil field without breaking sweat.

'Why pull a knife on you?' He threw the question back at me and went into first gear as we edged forward a few metres. 'Because you're there, Daniel,' he said. 'That's why!' His tone was big brotherish but I didn't mind because, at that moment, a big brother was exactly what I needed. 'Because you're there to be attacked and because *they can*!' We were moving and he explained some statistics, about how the people most likely to be attacked or murdered were the homeless, how of the homeless those most likely to be attacked or murdered were young men of my age. 'But you know all this, Daniel. You watch TV!'

'I don't seem to do much else.'

'So I'm boring you with a load of facts you already know.'

'I know all the facts, I've heard them all a hundred times but . . . but it wouldn't happen to me!'

'Daniel, do you really believe that?'

Five or six hours ago, I'd told myself the laws of the jungle just wouldn't hit me. In the space of hours, Danny-Nine-Lives had been reduced to the broke, bagless, homeless Danny.

'I've got a knife myself,' I told him, and as an afterthought, 'Or at least, I did have.' He looked interested but said nothing. 'I took it from the kitchen drawer before I left home. You know, just in case.' But he still said nothing.

'I put it at the bottom of my bag so I guess it's somewhere between here and California by now . . . along with all my other stuff.'

'A knife?'

'It was only an old kitchen knife with a wavy edge.

Just in case, like I said. It was made for cutting fruit and veg, not people!'

'But surely,' he said, 'the only people who carry knives are those who are prepared to use them.'

'Not this turkey . . .' I was sorry I'd mentioned the knife. 'It was a kitchen knife, black plastic handle, from IKEA.' I not only felt deeply sad and ashamed but could sense the cocktail of bad feeling settle on my face like a black sunset.

'Ah, c'mon, cheer up!' he laughed. 'Today's your lucky day, Daniel. Today, you met me! And today's my lucky day too. I came across you. I can't drive and film video at the same time.'

We were moving steadily, and, up ahead, there were vast spaces of open road.

'Still want to go to London?' he asked. 'Or would you like to stick around with me for a couple of days?'

'Where are we going, Luke?' I answered. He nodded down the line of traffic in the middle lane. 'We're following that!' *It* heaved out of the middle lane and into the left, streamers and flags hanging from its windows and roof and flapping in the breeze as it went.

It was a clapped out single decker bus, rust-coloured on the surface from bonnet to boot but decorated with enough wild-coloured paint to make it stand out as it hugged the hard shoulder and turned up the slip road, off the motorway, well over half a kilometre ahead of us. We weaved our way onto the hard shoulder, onto the track taken by the beaten-up bus. It was ploughing uphill and it seemed like a miracle it could even move.

'Get the video camera from the back seat,' he told me. 'Have you used one before?' he asked.

I had, but not one so expensive as this. I'd spent a joyous four hours with a camcorder at a family wedding recording the drunken antics of my bloodline, their obscure arguments, their declarations of undying love. Fiona, the bride, crying hysterically as the groom and best man slugged it out on the dance floor (Fiona was the cause). It was the height of fun.

Record, a red light came on. 'Keep it fixed on the bus, Daniel!'

'I can drive you know, Luke.' He didn't take me up on it, so I carried on trying to impress him. 'Yeah, my dad taught me to drive. My dad reckoned I was a natural.'

'Where'd you learn?'

'On a beach in Wales.'

'There's a bit of a difference between a beach in Wales and a busy motorway.'

'I've driven on a road as well.'

'Have you got a licence?' asked Luke.

'I'm too young to take the test.'

'Then I'd be grateful if you'd stick to the camcorder and leave me to drive.'

He slowed right down as we came onto the narrow country roads and I turned my eye to the lens and fixed on the back of the bus.

'Do you know the people in the bus?'

'Not personally. They're travelling people. The New Age brigade.'

I'd seen the travellers on TV, lots of times, having

murder with the cops when they wouldn't allow them near Stonehenge or some other ancient party venue.

'Why are we following them, Luke?' Travellers meant policemen and that I didn't need.

'Trust me!' he almost whispered. So I trusted him. 'Don't worry about the travellers or the cops or anyone else! It's going to be hunky-dory on the big bad globe, Daniel!' I believed him. I smiled to myself. I peered at the back of the lumbering bus through the lens of the camcorder. 'Hey! Hey, Luke, check out the back window of the bus!'

I zoomed in on the grime-ground glass and there, looking back at us was a child, a blond-haired boy with saucer sized blue eyes, eyes that seemed to make the dirt vanish and a face that reminded me of a Medieval paintings of a little angel. He raised a hand and waved and, with my free hand, I waved back. He smiled and pressed his face against the glass to get a closer look at us, and then a woman appeared at his side; she looked at us for a few moments and her face fell into a dozen or so creases. She was plainly upset by our presence and, picking up the boy, was soon away from the window.

'She thinks we're the law!' said Luke. 'She thinks we're the enemy!'

I then became aware of the narrowness of the road we were travelling and how broad the hedges on either side were, how tall and secretive, and that there was nothing behind us but a stretch of empty road and nothing ahead but a busload of people who thought we were the enemy. The bus made a sharp turn into the bank at the side, completely blocking the road and we were trapped in the rural equivalent of a dead end alley.

Luke stopped the Range Rover but kept the engine running.

'Luke, quickly, do a three-point turn and let's go back!'

'Calm down and keep filming!'

A man stepped down from the bus and half-walked, half-stomped his way into the middle of the road, directly in front of the Range Rover, It was as if he alone and his body could prevent the Range Rover from advancing another metre, as if he was a barrier between us and them.

My grandma (now dead), a Welsh woman with a thin face and a tendency not to laugh much, had a catch phrase. *Ugly as sin!* Many, many things, according to dear old Gran, were as ugly as sin. Sin stood before us, hands on hips and ready for a fight. I could almost hear my grandma's lilting voice, with its undertone of doom. 'My, he's as ugly as sin!'

'Get out, you snivelling pigs! Get out now before I drag you out!' He was an out and out Cockney, and – my, oh my! – he was as ugly as *sin*!

'Stay here, Daniel, I'll deal with it!' I didn't argue with him.

'Oi! You, turn that camera off before I stick it where it hurts!' No problem. I turned it off instantly and hid it from sight.

As Luke started talking with him – their conversation quiet, intense, their heads close – I watched the guy's face with morbid fascination. The lower half was covered with a dense shaggy beard, twisted at the ends into a dozen or so points, and the head crowned with a mat of collar length dreadlocks. His forehead jutted out like a caveman's and this overshadowed his eyes, which were brown, brown and wild and rimmed with black circles on a bloodshot sea of angry veins that reminded me of a mad alsatian's bulging eyeballs as it reared to bust its lead. The skin was scored and raised like a relief map of the moon, the legacy of a crop of recurring boils. His lips rolled this way and that and, if I hadn't been so nervous, I'd have felt sorry for him.

The blond kid appeared in the arms of the woman – his mum I assumed – who'd taken him from the back window, and our eyes met briefly. She looked right through me, so I pulled a funny face at the child and showed him two thumbs. He smiled and laughed back at me, raised a pair of tiny thumbs and I found myself feeling very sorry for him, growing up with a gang of dead beats like this.

Luke was talking and Sin was listening. His face fell still while Luke spoke quietly, staring as he did so into the long lost wilderness of the guy's face.

Then he laughed. He laughed, a full-bellied, open-throated laugh that rang around the hedges and sent a tribe of starlings straight up to the sky. Luke held out a hand and gargoyle features clasped it. The back window of the bus was ablaze with smiling faces. Even Sin looked better with a smile.

Luke threw an arm about his shoulders and drew him towards the Range Rover. I opened the door. 'Daniel, we've got our man!' said Luke. *We have?* I thought quietly. 'Daniel, meet Weasel!'

'Pleased to meet you, mate!' Weasel told me, as he swamped my hand in his, and peered into my eyes. 'This is the man we're making a film about!' Luke announced. So that was how he'd won him round. Luke had told Weasel what he wanted to hear.

Weasel was grinning at me. He had several teeth missing. He smelt like a wet bin on a warm day.

3

Vampires

We put together a cover story for the benefit of anyone who happened to take an interest in us. We stuck with our real names, Luke and Daniel. We were cousins and our mothers were sisters (lies, of course); he was a media student, making a fly-on-the-wall documentary about life on the road (which was true), or for Weasel's benefit, a documentary about Weasel's life on the road, and having finished my exams last summer (which was another porkie pie, the GCSEs were a little over two months away), I was helping him out. He was pushing nineteen years of age (the truth) and I was sixteen (two months short in reality). I tried out a whole pack of interesting details to buff up our story but he'd been quite firm. 'Keep it simple,' he'd said. 'Don't make up more than you need to. You've got to be a cross between Einstein and an elephant to lie properly.'

We parked on the edge of the field where Weasel had decided his people should set up for the night and, as darkness gathered in the sky, Luke and Weasel went for a walk because Mr Hygiene had something to get off his chest. I stretched out on the back seat and wondered what Mum thought when she found the note I'd Blu-tack'd to the bathroom mirror over sixteen hours earlier.

Mum,

You said I made the place a misery with my sour face so I've decided to do you a favour by leaving your house for good. By the way, I overheard you and Aunt Gemma in the kitchen two Fridays ago (when you drank the best part of a bottle of gin between you, remember?), and you're right. I had no idea I was an unplanned pregnancy and that contraceptives were useless back then. But I've also got no idea how Dad could stoop so low to have anything to do with you in the first place . . . his French girlfriend is much more attractive and interesting than you could ever have been!
Danny

I massaged my temples to fend off a gathering headache and wondered if she'd been in touch with school? (St. Patrick's College, run by Christian Brothers, a boys only school, that constantly stank of sweaty socks, floor polish and incense.)

The last lad to do a runner, Clive Carter, lasted three days in Blackpool before being roped in by the law, drunk and disorderly, and shipped back to Merseyside in a pool of his own vomit.

I wondered, had she been in touch with the police and if she was going to give them a picture of me for the Missing Persons poster, I hoped to God it wasn't the one with me in that crappy velvet jacket at Fiona's wedding. Had it affected her usual routine, me running away? It was Tuesday night and she worked as a waitress, Tuesdays, at a Steak House down by the Pier Head. It was almost worth a phone call to find out.

Outside, the lighter patches of sky were rapidly becoming swamped in heavier hues of black and blue, and with the darkness, Weasel's 'Family' (his word, not mine) came alive like a pack of vampires; and in the clinking of cider bottles and the crackling of open fires, far away, a bird of some sort, maybe an owl, maybe not, called out three times and then fell silent.

The night was tinted hot orange from the rising flames and the whole experience was like a dream. *This is just a dream . . . this is not a dream . . .* the words came back and haunted me like a song I couldn't get out of my head.

I sat up and there, on the bonnet, was the blond boy I'd first seen at the back of the bus. He pressed his hands and nose into the glass, a mist forming on the windscreen close to his mouth. He was two, maybe three years old, and as I watched him, I wished that he was in a house, in a bed, safe asleep, with normal parents to tuck him in.

As I sat up to my full height, I spoke to him in my best children's TV presenter voice. 'Hello there, mate!' I chimed, and he immediately started crying, sliding help-lessly down and hitting the ground with a thud.

I jumped out, finding a stick of gum in my pocket which I unwrapped and handed to him. It did the trick and soothed him down. I asked, 'What's your name then, lad?' I knelt down beside him and smiled.

'Kyle Wolf!'

'That's a nice name,' I lied and reached out to pick him up. A pair of worn-out tears fell silently down his angelic face and, as I took his hands in mine, the kid lashed out with his foot catching me on the side of the chin with his boot, like a good left hook. A light flashed – inside my head or out, I couldn't tell.

'Ow! Ow! Ow!' I danced about. Kyle giggled joyfully, got to his feet unaided, and wandered back towards the heat and fires at the heart of the site, turning back only to wave at me and shout, ''Bye 'bye, Mister Mister.'

''Bye 'bye, Kyle Kyle!' I called, rubbing my face and tasting blood inside my mouth. I watched his tiny shambling form melt into the darkness between the fires, and I hoped he'd be all right.

'Are you OK?' Luke spoke, like an echo from the morning, and again, he seemed to come from nowhere. I looked to the sound of his voice and a white light flashed. Luke smiled and took another photograph before slipping the camera in his jacket pocket. 'Want me to take one of you?' I asked, but he shook his head.

'Come on, Daniel.' He was already getting into the driver's seat. 'I've been talking to Weasel, the guy's a crackpot! He's got baubles for brains!'

All thoughts of home dissolved as Luke turned the ignition and I climbed on board, catching a large dose of his infectious laughter.

'Where are we off to?' I asked.

'A hotel. We really don't want to hang around this lot longer than we have to. I haven't got a great deal of money, Daniel, but seeing as tonight's your first night away . . .' I was delighted to be getting away. Kyle excepted – the Weasel's people gave me a massive dose of the creeps. 'Tomorrow, we camp!'

'We don't have to go to a hotel.'

'We've got a big day tomorrow. You'll need a good night's sleep.'

'What's happening tomorrow?'

'We'll talk about it later, Daniel.'

★ ★ ★

We were in the car park at the front of a mock Tudor country hotel.

Luke looked at the camcorder and tapes, and glanced at me. 'Do you think they'll be all right out here?' I threw my suede over them on the back seat.

'We're in the middle of nowhere,' I said, as we walked to the main door, and suddenly he laughed. 'What is it?' I asked, as we walked into the White Stag Hotel.

'Weasel thinks the world's on the brink of a big eco-logical disaster, a nuclear accident or something. This year, he told me it's going to happen on Halloween, the jerk. But, Daniel. The joke of it is . . .' Luke laughed so hard he couldn't get to the punch line for a moment. 'Weasel reckons the only people who'll survive are him and whoever he sees fit to save.'

'And how's he going to manage that?'

'He says he knows a magical cave under the ground, near Stonehenge where he can sit out the worst of it and when it's all over, he's going to come out with his followers and be the King of the World, start off a brand new human race, formed in the likeness of his image.'

'Well, if that's true, super models are going to be a thing of the past.'

When we approached the desk, the owner, Mrs Sarah Blackwell, an addled-looking woman, maybe thirty, maybe ninety years old, eyed us with suspicion. She insisted, in the nicest possible way, on payment up front for the room. Luke obliged her with a quartet of tenners and a request for a table in the restaurant. It was a good moment. She smiled. Bitterly.

Doubling up as waitress, she came to our table and, before I could speak, Luke ordered, 'Vegetarian lasagne, twice please, chips and a side salad. You want a side salad, Daniel?' I shook my head and handed the menu back.

I'd seen steak on the menu and had wanted that, but what could I say? I'd even smelt steak from the kitchen near the table where we sat, and seen steak delivered to the table next to us where a middle-aged couple were sawing away with steak knives. Luke caught me looking over at them.

'You didn't want steak, did you?' he asked.

'No, I want vegetarian lasagne, Luke.'

'It's just, I don't eat meat and . . .' He leaned in closer. 'The smell of meat, it knocks me sick. I can't eat when it's on the same table. I feel funny them eating it on the next table.' I nodded. 'The way they treat the animals, it's barbaric. Do you know anything about the meat industry, Daniel?'

I'd seen it on TV, life and death on the abattoir floor

and I agreed, the whole set-up was a disgrace. But I had a problem. Ten minutes after the documentary credits had rolled on the box, I couldn't connect the cow hanging on the meat hook with the burger in the bun.

'Yeah, I'm nearly vegetarian myself. I hardly ever eat meat. I hate the way animals are treated.'

'No point in being a nearly, Daniel. Why not go the whole way?'

I eyed his leather jacket and was tempted to ask him the same question; but I didn't. I just shrugged and smiled. He buttered some bread and handed it to me. *You're a bossy hypocrite*, I thought. I paused over the bread and bit the inside of my mouth which was already cut from Kyle's kung fu kick. Blood leaked across my tongue which served me right because I was ripping him to shreds in my head while I nodded and smiled and ate *his* bread.

'About tomorrow. Weasel told me there's a fox hunt not far from here.'

'A fox hunt?' Now there was a clear-cut issue. For a long time, I'd wanted to do something about blood sports but never got round to much more than signing petitions and feeling angry. 'How near's near?'

'An estate called Dunvegan Hall, ten miles from here. Weasel's going to sabotage it. He wants us to film it. Any problem with that?'

'No problem at all! I'd like to get a couple of redcoats and crack their skulls open! I can't tell you, Luke, how I hate them. I'd like to set a pack of dogs on them and see if they still called it sport.'

'I've touched a raw nerve,' said Luke.

I hadn't noticed Mrs Blackwell arriving with our meals but the look she gave told me she'd heard me taking off and she was plainly one of the country crew. Luke pulled a face: *You've done it now, sonny!* The plates almost splintered as she slammed them onto the table and hoofed back to the kitchen.

Luke paused over his food and calmly said, 'There's a baseball bat in the Rover. Tomorrow, we'll crack at least one head open!' As he tucked into his pasta, there was a sudden buzzing of panic behind my ribs that killed my appetite stone dead. Violent talk was one thing . . . 'Come on, Daniel, eat up!' I lifted my fork but it was like a dead weight in my hand. 'You see, I agree with you,' said Luke. He clenched a fist and made a swiping motion, low against the table, for my eyes only. I stabbed the lasagne and scrambled around my head for a way out. And then Luke said, 'Then again, tomorrow, we'll just record what goes on. Maybe that's our best role. Just that. No violence.'

I was so relieved I could have strutted around the room like a knock-kneed chicken. When it came down to it, I was no good at violence, and I had a vested interest in keeping the lowest of possible profiles. I needed to be arrested like I needed a Wonderbra and a tattooed forehead.

'We'll film Weasel, and film from a safe distance.' He smiled at me and said, 'Tomorrow belongs to me!'

'Tomorrow then; sounds good,' I said, disguising the heaviest sigh of relief.

'Tomorrow it is.'

4

Morning

I woke up during the night, from a very bad dream, at first not remembering a single image from it, but filled with a jaw-locking fear, and wondering where on earth I was. I felt paralysed with confusion and, all my senses in overdrive, I whispered, I wondered, 'Where am I?' And I wondered, What am I doing here? But there was only silence and dense dark and the terror of having slipped into a black hole at the furthest point in outer space.

I then heard Luke's shallow breathing not far away and a chain of ideas locked into each other. Luke, hotel, countryside, motorway, runaway, and the dream crystallised inside my head.

I was running, chased at highest speed, my face pressed close to the ground as I pelted along the grass verge of the motorway, the sound of stampeding feet behind me, the certainty that the gap was closing quickly, heavy hooves, deadly paws behind me, and ahead, on an embankment, a deep hole was waiting for me. I was running at full stretch, my back legs almost lifting me high from the ground, my front feet working to keep me on line and heading for the hole. But I could feel the breath of the hounds and the loose phlegm that swept from their jowls as the head of the pack got within a tooth's width of the tip of my tail, and the gaping hole, and the hope of safety, was suddenly further away than it had ever been. The hunter's bugle rang out in triumph as the hounds pounced, savaged me to the ground with their dagger-sharp teeth and tore flannels of fur from my flesh in eager mouthfuls.

I drifted in and out of sleep during what was left of the night and lay still, dozing here and there, through the restless hours till morning came crawling through the gap between the curtains, and Luke came into the room through a narrow gap in the doorway, returning to the bed I hadn't seen him leaving.

★ ★ ★

It was like arriving in the village of the dead. Smoke drifted from what was left of last night's fires along with half a skipload of empty booze bottles, scattered across the field. Luke eyed the mess, shook his head and whispered, 'Pigs!'

'Where'd you go last night, Luke?'

'Last night?' he looked at me, perplexed. 'Nowhere.'

'I woke up around dawn, you were coming into the room from the corridor.'

'Oh that. Yeah, I heard a noise in the corridor. I wondered what it was. I went to check it.'

'And what was it?'

'Nothing.'

'Central heating pipes, maybe?' I thought out loud.

He shrugged, said, 'Maybe,' and nodded to the largest

of the tents, the one that looked least likely to blow away or fall down. Something moved. 'Get it on video!' said Luke so I started the camcorder, as Weasel emerged from the tent, bleary-eyed, half-dead, doing his pants up.

'Weasel! C'mon, man!' Luke clearly wanted away and quickly with it.

Weasel followed us to the Rover, opened the back door and climbed in behind me, bringing with him his own designer cocktail of smells: vintage body odour and long forgotten teeth, lingering food and a code of hygiene lost behind too many years on the road and too many miles from running water.

I tried not to shrink away from Weasel, as his claw-like hand, with its layers of grime and astrological tattoos, reached over to me.

'And you are?' He was baiting me. I could feel the contempt in his voice as it hit the back of my neck. Luke hit first gear and we were away.

I turned and clasped his hand, 'I am who I am!'

In the distance, Kyle's mum came out from a tent, agitated, waving her arms as if someone had set her feet on fire. She ran a few metres after us, but we swung through a gap in the hedge and were away. Without thinking, I'd filmed her doing her little war dance. I turned it off and faced the front.

'Am I heading in the right direction?' asked Luke.

'Keep going, I'll tell you where to turn!' Weasel spoke from the depths of the other world he inhabited. 'Hey, Liverpool . . .' He spoke to me properly now.

'Yes, London?'

29

'What's your name?'

'Daniel!'

'Daniel in the lions' den yet? Like Daniel in the Bible went into the lions' den and the lions wouldn't hurt Daniel. What's it like in the lions' den?'

'Yeah, well, I went into the lions' den, once . . . at Chester Zoo. I gave one of them my sandwiches. It was very grateful.'

'No, Daniel,' Weasel breathed. 'You're now in the lions' den.'

'What are you on, Weasel?'

'Daniel, I'm on *everything*!'

And for the next few miles, we listened as Weasel sang a selection of songs he'd written himself, songs rich in bum rhyming lyrics and instantly forgettable tunes, music from the juke box in Hell.

When he grew tired of singing, he told us of how he'd been the commander-in-chief of all the major civil disobedience gigs, tree-felling, live cattle exports, global capitalism riots, which was why the government had a contract out on him.

When he grew tired of his heroic exploits, he yawned, farted and fell asleep for the rest of the journey.

We dropped him off at a cross-roads, near Dunvegan, where the hunt was due to start. He told Luke to pick him up at the same spot later on. Luke said, 'Yeah, OK!' yet smiled at me and I guessed Weasel had a long walk ahead of him.

Through a line of roadside trees we could see the back of Dunvegan Hall and a crowd of protesters held back by a line of police at a fenced boundary of the land. As we travelled down the road, saboteurs, some in pairs, some alone, were roaming the green fields and I thought back on Weasel's words, about Daniel in the lions' den. Maybe he meant this quiet English countryside, this was the lions' den. Then again, maybe he was just talking through his backside.

I took it all down on video tape as we carried on, towards the gate at the rear of the Hall, now splendid and elegant in the morning sun. The hired hands, the dog handlers, the collaborators and the redcoats hung around on horseback, gathering like night in an old time horror movie.

'Nervous at all?' asked Luke. But I made no reply. I turned off the camcorder which now felt clammy where I held it against my shoulder with my hand, and for a moment, the world around me went quiet, dissolved by the mind's eye, and I was there again, on the big screen in the multi-screen cinema back home, half a metre taller than I was in real life, arms roped in muscle, eyes narrow with determination, chin square and set, the video camera a portable rocket launcher. Luke, half-man, half-machine, drove through an exploding minefield, and we were super heroes, untouched by firepower, chasing our enemies into their own lines.

'They were on a mission!' An American voice, steel and stone, filled my head, while my enormous chest muscles rippled as we thundered relentlessly into the haze of a corpse-littered war zone. 'The Two who just wouldn't take it any more . . .' Then the macho voice-over evaporated, and the real world became solid once more, as fresh lines of sunlight fell though the green canopy above us, and a blackbird, or something, sang quite merrily at the top of its range.

A bowler-hatted hunt steward flagged us down as we headed to the gate. He carried a clipboard and marched towards us with military precision. Luke rolled the window down and leaned out. 'It's Mr Bowler Hat!' Luke sneered as he approached us.

'Are you on the guest list?' Bowler Hat sounded just like the father in a farmer's daughter joke.

'No, we're not on the guest list!' Luke suddenly sounded different, like he belonged inside the stately home. 'We're filmmakers, and we were wondering, any chance of letting us in, just for a few minutes or so!'

Bowler Hat laughed, all teeth and attitude, straight into Luke's face and muttered something about, 'Filmmakers? Muckrakers!'

Luke held onto Bowler Hat's gaze, and his grin faded as his eyes delved deeper into Luke's. 'Say yes if you can,' Luke said. 'Say no if you must but don't laugh at us!' Behind his even tone, Luke was raging and Bowler Hat bristled like an alley cat.

'Not on the guest list?' said Bowler Hat. 'Then you'd better clear off before there's any trouble.'

'We don't want trouble,' Luke pronounced, turning to me and laughing. I nodded in agreement. 'We're peace-loving lads.' Luke reached out and shook hands with Bowler Hat, taking him by surprise.

'Turn round and follow the road back the way you came!'

The Hat was trying to pull away, but Luke held onto his hand and said, 'We'll just get going!' He mocked the guy, copying him with uncanny ease, the way he picked and spoke his words, imitating his voice and facial expressions and when Bowler Hat realised what was going on, Luke let go of his hand.

'You'd better get away from here!' threatened the Hat, producing a mobile phone like a cowboy would a gun, 'or I'll see to it you get a good hiding!'

Luke put the Rover into reverse and called, 'Don't piss your pants, Bowler Hat, we're on our way! But you really shouldn't have laughed at us.' Luke threw this at him, as he did a sudden three-point turn, not giving the Hat a chance to answer. 'See you soon, promise!' Luke spat the words at him and drove down the road.

I held my silence for a while before asking, 'Are you OK, Luke?'

'He shouldn't have laughed!' There was something very grim about the way he looked for a moment and I was stuck for words until he hummed a few bars of a song I thought I'd heard before but couldn't place.

He breathed a few words in line with a thin melody and then fell into a solemn silence.

'What's that?' I asked, trying to lighten the mood a little.

'That? It's just a song.'

★ ★ ★

33

We broke onto the estate, following a small group of protesters running in the general direction of the Hall. 'Let's go!' said Luke, heading after the group. As I followed him, a ball of tension spread from the pit of my stomach, rolling this way one moment, that way the next, while an unstoppable itching sensation developed just beneath the surface of my scalp.

We stopped near a cluster of trees, oak trees I think, oak or beech maybe, but trees with plenty of branches and very comfortable places on which to perch way up above the ground.

'Luke,' I said, inspired by a way of finding an even greater distance between us and the action, without coming across as completely wet. I pointed to the tree-tops. 'Let's get a bird's-eye view of things!'

And to my relief, he said, 'Good idea, Daniel!'

I stuffed the camcorder down my T-shirt and said, 'Watch and follow!' Two good handholds and a gnarl near the base of the tree was enough to send me off up the bark, clutching with my hands and looping my legs across the branches. 'You won't fall,' I egged him on, pulling him up by the arms and resting my weight down on his hands to secure him. He wriggled his way onto a branch just below me and took a series of deep breaths.

The view was excellent and everything had a place, like some cracked game of chess. The redcoats grouped to start the hunt with dogs and servants, the protesters waiting for them, held by a line of policemen while across the fields, saboteurs sprayed the grass with aerosols, scattering false scents to fool the hounds. I took the camcorder, pressed record and zoomed in on the hunting party where Bowler Hat took a glass of wine from a tray of drinks, and laughed and smiled and chatted away.

'Check out the hunting party, Luke. Your best mate's there.'

'Oh yes,' said Luke. 'And smiling like the man with no brain! A man with no brain?' he went on. 'Maybe that's how he'll end up. Well, I'm glad he's happy now. You never know what's round the corner.'

I was about to seek a little further explanation when a roar of anger rose from the crowd.

The hunt got off. The police stood their ground against a surge from the protestors as the horses, hounds and riders streamed off in our direction. It was hard to keep up with the action and keep balanced and I nearly lost the the camcorder when Luke cried out, 'Over there, Daniel!'

A solitary red fox appeared in the middle of nowhere and found itself facing a tide of death. The hunting party went up a gear as the hounds sprang into action. The fox was heading towards the east where the sun shone brightly and for a moment the image through the lens was drowned out by the dense light. The sun then faded and I could see again through the lens.

The dogs at the front of the pack turned quickly, all informed by one and the same instinct, and started heading towards us. It was the first time I'd ever seen a real live fox; it looked young, and it was running towards the trees for its life. I wanted to turn the camera off but

I couldn't; as the fox sped closer, its face came into focus, its nose, its eyes, its inner terror.

They were closing on the fox, the dogs were probably going to corner it in the trees around us. I closed my eyes and, in a flash, saw everything through the fox's eyes, just as I had done in my dream, the ground rising up as my spirit sprinted with her.

I opened my eyes and pinned the camera onto the oncoming riders, their faces red with excitement in the morning sun, their eyes, ears, noses and mouths, their heads protected by hard black hats; men, women, and a girl of my age or thereabouts. She looked blank, not happy, not sad or excited, but she was there and she was one of them.

Below us, the barking grew to fever pitch, and I knew that the inevitable had happened. The fox cried, cried like a battered child, as they fell on her with tooth and claw in the shadows of the trees. Silence fell around us while the redcoats stopped a little short of where we were. A numbness spread inside me, a deadening of feeling, a quickening of my heart.

'How quick the dogs, how stupid the fox,' a voice gurgled from the ground. And Luke spoke, too, beneath his breath, but I couldn't quite hear his words.

I got close-ups of their faces, smiles, self-satisfaction, chuckling happily as they waited. I scanned the group and settled on the girl. Someone called her name, 'Kathy!' She turned and shook her head. Were there tears in her eyes or was it a trick of the light? She removed her hat to reveal a mass of dark hair, tied tightly into a knot. I panned the camera away as the dogs emerged from the trees to a round of applause with the blood-stained corpse of the fox-cub.

'What's this?' I asked. A child of eight or nine years was led forward by the hand.

Luke replied, 'They're blooding the kid!' The Master of the hunt dipped a cloth in the fox's open wounds and smeared blood on the boy's face.

I looked away and turned off the camcorder. Not only couldn't I record this, I couldn't even watch.

Luke spoke softly, his voice lost in a rustling of leaves.

'What was that, Luke?' I whispered.

'*Blood*, I said . . . if this is what they want, this is exactly what they'll get!'

5

Video Nasty?

As afternoon dissolved into early evening, I was so tired I could have slept in an open grave and when we trudged back to the Range Rover, it was a huge relief just to sit down and do nothing other than close my eyes.

'Tired?' asked Luke. 'Sit here for a while and rest, Daniel.'

Happily, I closed my eyes but as soon as darkness filled my head a stream of vivid pictures jumped up without order or warning, the dogs with the dead fox and the face of the boy as it was daubed with blood. And Kathy. If I'd seen her walking down a street, I'd never have guessed it of her.

'Leave you here for bit, Daniel? You can catch up on some sleep.'

'Where're you going?'

'A walk.'

'OK . . . Luke. Thanks.'

'Sweet dreams.'

As he wandered off, he sang that same song again, as he made his way through the hanging branches that hid the car from the road. I lay down on the seats and made a pillow of my forearms. My heart was beating like I'd just run up a dozen sets of steps, just like it did when I went into the school hall to sit exams, just like I was supposed to be doing in a couple of months. But I didn't want to think of home or school. I'd only been away thirty-six hours but it felt like thirty-six months, and I told myself firmly I wasn't going back. Ever? Ever. Ever . . .

Kathy came back to my mind. Luke had called her all the wicked little cows under the sun. I'd nodded and uttered the odd half-hearted, 'I guess so.' But, in the quietness, I guessed she was only doing it for a quiet life at home. Then, for a moment, I didn't think anything at all, but heard a voice deep inside me murmur, *If she was a dog you wouldn't be looking for excuses for her!*

When I awoke, night was forming between the spaces in the trees and Luke still wasn't back. I sat up and reached for the door handle. It was locked. My eyes drifted to the ignition but there was no sign of the keys and I realised I was locked inside.

Out of nowhere, a long buried memory of being accidentally locked in a garden shed when I was two years old scrambled itself to the very front of my mind and panic invaded me from all angles, engaged itself in a quickfire banter inside my head. *What was up?* Something was horribly wrong. *What's Luke done?* Locked you in!

I touched the windows to probe for some non-existent weakness and with each passing moment desperate fears zig-zagged around my brain. I'd never liked cramped spaces, nor locked doors, nor lights that went out on landings through the cracks in bedroom doors. *Just a dream, not a dream . . .* echoed through my mind, as Luke walked through the shrubs, smiling, peering at me through the growing darkness like some supernatural woodland creature.

It was at that moment I saw the keys on the floor by the clutch and in that instant the hobgoblins and bogeymen scuttled back into the shadows at the edges of my memory. 'Sleep OK?' he asked me, opening the driver's door.

I'd woken up and panicked and felt rather stupid as he picked up the keys from the floor where he'd left them (and I hadn't seen them) and dropped a carrier bag of fruit, chocolate and canned drinks into my lap with a cheery, 'Help yourself, Daniel.' I felt myself blush. He was kindness itself rolled up into one person, yet only moments earlier, in my mounting panic, I'd accused him in my head of locking me in. I took an apple Tango from the bag and drank slowly as he whistled the tune of the song he'd hummed earlier. Then he sang one line over and over. Again and again.

'You like that song, don't you?' I said to him; but he didn't answer. We turned down a narrow lane which was just about wide enough for us and I wondered if I was going a bit crazy, for accusing Luke, in my mind, of locking me in. Just about crazy enough to think that and quite sane enough to feel guilty about it.

'Guess who I saw, just before?' he asked.

'I don't know. No idea. Who?'

'Bowler Hat.'

'Did he see you?' I flushed hot, then went suddenly cold. Luke shook his head.

'He was going into a pub, The Cat and Fiddle, with

a load of people from the hunt.' Luke fell silent, as if he was expecting me to speak. He glanced at me. He was waiting and I didn't know what he wanted me to say.

I bit my thumbnail and muttered, 'So was he still wearing that stupid hat then?' Luke nodded. He was still waiting.

He wanted me to say something more definite than this, so I tried to oblige with, 'What a jerk! I don't know what he thought he was laughing at.'

'That's what I reckoned, Daniel, that's it. What the hell was he laughing at us for when he wants to have a good look at himself?' He didn't sound as angry as he had done before, but he was *going on a bit*. 'Maybe he needs to be taught a lesson?' The question hung between us like an embarrassing odour.

'About what?' I asked, trying to clear that air.

'About manners. Get the camcorder ready and mute the sound!'

I lifted the camcorder to my shoulder and pointed it directly in the path we were travelling, down a narrow village street where a string of coloured lights swayed in the wind between two trees and up in the distance was a pub, The Cat and Fiddle. Luke slowed right down and pulled over, a little way up the road from the pub and in the lengthening shadows of an ancient-looking church that was lit from the ground by huge uplighters.

'Keep the tape rolling!' Luke spoke without feeling, with a voice that could have been borrowed from a zombie. 'Keep it on the front door of that pub. They're all in there. All of them.'

My throat was drying up fast. 'What've you got in mind?'

'Observing, recording, putting things straight for the record, that sort of thing.' Luke spoke the words as if he was passing on a deep and ancient secret and secrets were a thing I had a deep dislike of. Somehow or other, other people's secrets had a very bad habit of getting me bollocked on other people's behalf.

The door of the pub opened and a blast of laughter and chatter volleyed out into the hovering darkness. There was a pause, no sign of anyone leaving and then, as if by some bad voodoo, out strolled Bowler Hat, laughing, as he made his way out alone into the darkness.

'There he is. It is him, isn't it?' asked Luke, gripping my arm.

'It's definitely him,' I agreed. There was a flop of grey hair hanging down from the back of his hat and brushing the collar of his green tweed jacket. I felt myself attacked by a legion of nervous giggle demons, as Bowler Hat staggered a little down the road and started undoing his pants to relieve himself in the alleyway between a post office and a square brick shop selling guns and fishing rods. The Hat looked back, this way and that, and, thinking he wasn't being watched, dipped into the alley.

'I hope he doesn't stand too near the wall or the splashback'll spray the front of his trousers!' Luke's voice was alive again but his eyes were quite dead.

And I laughed, short, sharp, nervous gasps of laughter which made the camcorder rock on my shoulder, yet beneath this, a deep voice within me whispered, *Get out and walk away!* I laughed harder to drown the voice but it came back louder again. I ignored it and laughed even louder, and the voice fell silent. Luke laughed and I laughed, like I'd done when Simon Butcher (a bully, with learning difficulties, who used to go to my primary school) chased me across the street and was knocked down and killed by a black Ford Orion.

'What are we going to do to him?' I asked, as if I was setting up the punch line of a playground joke. I felt a terrific thirst and my teeth were welding together.

Luke turned the ignition and the engine sighed into life. 'Just keep the camera trained on him!'

Bowler Hat stepped out, sideways, fumbling with his trousers and coughing. His shoulders arched, as if a shiver had just passed down his spine, and he strolled down the sloping street as Luke took the handbrake off and we followed. He walked in a drunken zig-zag down the middle of the road while Luke steered towards him. At that moment in time, Bowler Hat was in the worst place possible, on the driver's side of Luke's Range Rover. The incline of the street seemed to pull us after Bowler Hat and Luke began singing, putting words to the tune he hummed and whistled a lot.

Luke took a breath. 'Keep it on him, Daniel!' We were free-wheeling down the street, the only sound the crunch of the tyres against the tarmac and Luke's window sliding down.

Bowler Hat seemed totally unaware as we stole up on him. There was no one about, I told myself, whatever else, no one else was there, and the camcorder was moving in on a big rear view close-up of the Hat.

Bowler Hat turned, very very slightly at the sound of the voice, but not in time to avoid the full swing of the baseball bat that Luke cracked against the back of his head. There was a noise, like an indoor firework dying on itself and the weight of his body slamming down on the road. Luke pulled over, snatched the camcorder from my feeble and trembling grip and ordered me, 'Get the hat! Get the hat!'

I jumped out and tore across the street where the bowler hat rolled around, close to the body, turning in on a decreasing circle, stopping a short way from his head. He gurgled in the back of his throat and, although his eyes were wide open, I knew he couldn't see; he was breathing through his mouth and it was as if he was drowning in thin air. I knew the sound. He'd swallowed his tongue.

I reached into his mouth and pulled the stiff tongue back; air poured down his windpipe and I laid him on his side in the recovery position. Luke gave a short blast on the horn, the words *Get the hat! Get the hat!* lurking deep in its tone, urging me on.

I picked up his hat and glared at him as if he was an alien, like he had no right to be there, an uninvited guest in the worst of all possible dreams. I reached out to touch, to check my eyes were not fooling me, to see if he was OK! His outbreath breezed over my hand, my fingers clenched tightly. I looked up. Luke was filming. I looked into the eye of the camera. 'Daniel, get in the bloody car now!' I obeyed, jumped into the passenger seat, clutching the bowler hat.

The giggle demons were chasing themselves around each fibre of my brain, as Luke turned the camcorder off. I sounded like a pig on the sharp end of a dagger but from the neck down I was numb with misery and shock. Luke swopped me the camcorder for the hat and propped it on his head as we sped away.

'Better clear off before there's any trouble!' Luke's impersonation of the Hat's voice was perfect, like he'd transplanted his vocal cords into his own throat. 'That's sorted him out!' It was uncanny, like the voice had been stolen from the core of the Hat's being, like a piece of loose skin, and grafted into Luke.

He slowed right down, without a hint of nerves, slipping into a sing-song of Bowler Hat's speaking voice. ''Bye'bye, Bowler Hat, Bowler Hat, 'bye 'bye!' And he threw the hat through the open window and into a field, like a frisbee.

I was completely silenced by it all and my face was in my hands.

'You OK, Daniel?' Suddenly, Luke sounded like himself again, the model of kindness, the heart and soul of friendly concern.

'Don't use that voice again.'

'Did it upset you?'

'It's weird, it's horribly . . .' Words failed me. 'Please don't do it again. It gives me the creeps.'

'Hey, I'm a good mimic, Daniel, that's all, and I'm

sorry if it bothers you! I was only trying to make a joke, to amuse you.'

I took another canned drink from the bag and found I could hardly open it, I was trembling so completely. When the can finally gave way to my pressing and prodding, I took several short sips and felt like my head was caving in from the centre of the brain outwards.

'Don't joke like that, Luke!'

He held his hands up from the wheel in a grand gesture of surrender to my wishes and shrugged, 'Whatever you say, Daniel, whatever you say!'

6

Night Vision

It took Luke less than two minutes to throw up the tubes and canvas of his sand and yellow coloured tent. We were totally alone on the field and I was feeling dead guilty. If anyone had seen me, they'd have looked into my eyes and seen the mounting shame inside. Luke whistled his favourite tune (which was really starting to get on my wick now), breaking off to tell me, breezily, 'This tent'll last forever. It's called a North Face MTN-24 and it cost £399. It's the sort of tent that'd do you up Mount Everest or in the middle of a storm but it only weighs as much as four bags of sugar.' He stopped. 'OK, I shouldn't have smacked Bowler Hat! I'm sorry. I can't turn the clock back but I promise you I won't do anything like that again. I can't say fairer than that. I just lost my rag with him. I gave in to a very bad urge. He'll have a sore head for a few days. That's all!'

Was I overreacting to what had happened? Was I turning a quick smack on the head into a major attack? People got all sorts of knocks to the head and were fine afterwards. I shrugged and nodded, 'The guy got what he deserved!'

'Yeah!' Luke nodded. 'Come on, let's try and get some sleep.'

As I followed him into his expensive dome-shaped

tent, I had the strangest idea: we were twins returning to a womb and as he fastened up the zip, we were gradually wrapped in one and the same darkness.

Pain edged its way into my sleep. Somewhere between midnight and daybreak, I woke slowly and took stock of my body, the rock inside my head, and my mounting sense of gloom. My nose was blocked. As I swallowed another mouthful of heavy air, my throat seized up; I coughed, and spluttered like a clapped-out moped trying to start up on a cold morning.

But it was a chilly night in March and the coldness was all confined to the whispering chills that tripped through my bones. Oh, lucky me! What every runaway needs most. 'Flu and a chest infection! If I'd been at home, I'd have been right into the medicine cabinet for a Lemsip and straight in front of the gas fire.

'Daniel? Are you OK?' He sat up suddenly. 'What's the matter?' He sounded sorry for me, and very concerned. 'Are you cold, Daniel? Here!'

He'd tuned right in to the way I felt. He reached across the darkness and handed me the sweater he'd rolled up for a pillow.

Even though I felt like the inside of an upright freezer, there was a film of sweat spreading across my forehead. I was developing a megadrive headache. I took the sweater from him and clutched it to myself.

'I don't feel too good.'

'You don't sound too good.'

I shifted my weight around to try and get comfortable

but, in moving, I felt like my arms and legs had been pumped with a dozen packets of Angel Delight.

He flicked on a torch and shone it just beneath my eyes. 'You're sweating,' he said as he sat at my feet. He watched me closely, very closely for some moments, his face a map of shifting shadows that would have been sinister had he not whispered, 'Take it easy, Daniel.' It was the kindest voice I'd ever heard. 'I know, I know,' he said, as if talking to himself. 'We'll go to Oxford, get a hotel. I'll take you there in the morning. It'll be light in a couple of hours, we'll go there and take a room.'

'But it costs money,' I replied, even though I could think of nowhere I'd rather be than in a comfortable bed with a TV set for when I was feeling a little better. 'I'll just stay here in this tent till it passes.' I lay back, using the sweater for a pillow and praying he wouldn't agree.

'Oh no, I insist, you must stay in a hotel while you're ill. Anyway, like I said, we aren't loaded but if money becomes a real problem we'll just steal some.'

I was too weak and tired to work out whether he was joking or not but even if he was being deadly serious I was feeling too sorry for myself to care. The pain in my head made my eyes close but I could still feel him staring at me. I peered over; he was gazing at me in torchlight.

'I don't know if this is a good time to ask, Daniel, but . . . No, I'll ask in the morning . . .'

'Go ahead, ask me now.'

'Why did you run away from home?'

'Because . . .' There were many reasons but one overwhelming idea. 'Because if I'd stayed at home another day, I'd have murdered my mother, strangled her or something worse even.'

'You hate your mother that much.' He didn't sound at all surprised. I nodded but suddenly all the long gone good times at home flooded back, vivid and real and it just didn't bear thinking about.

'I know what you mean. I did a runner myself when I was fourteen; my mum and me, we couldn't look at each other without snarling like a pair of Pit Bulls. I knew the moment I saw you, back in the service station, I thought, that lad's on his toes. I thought, I know what he's going through.'

'You felt sorry for me then?'

'No. Not exactly sorry. I wished . . . I wish when I'd done a runner, someone'd stopped me from going to London. I didn't want you to go there. Anyway, I'm glad you're here. And I don't feel sorry for you. If I didn't like you I'd have given you a tenner and told you to take good care of yourself.'

His friendship was like a physical force reaching inside me and making me feel stronger, better. A smile broke out on my face, a smile I couldn't hold back.

'What happened?' I asked. 'What happened to you in London?'

'I'll tell you some other time.' The wind heaved and sighed down on the tent, but I felt safe, not locked in, not buried alive.

'Daniel?'

'Yes?'

'Who's Pascale?' Luke asked.

I hadn't mentioned Pascale to him, in fact I hadn't mentioned anything about my home or family life that I could think of. I searched his face in the torchlight and saw a questioning look in his eyes.

'You mentioned her in your sleep, last night. And just before. About half an hour ago. You must've been dreaming, you were talking in your sleep, kept mentioning Pascale.'

'Pascale? She's the chief reason my parents divorced, two years ago.'

'Daddy's piece on the side?'

'Daddy's piece on the side!'

'So what's she like, Daniel?'

'She's got this long blonde hair that hangs down to the base of her back and she looks like a model. Like something off the front of a magazine. She's got this pouting red gash of a mouth. She's got curves to kill for. She's just gorgeous. Oh yes, and she's very clever as well. She speaks three languages and works as a personal assistant to some high-ranking French copper. That's how my dad met her. He's a copper, well, he used to be a copper. He gave it all up, including Mum, to go and live with Pascale in Paris.'

'How come your dad went to France in the first place?'

'He went to collar some dope dealer from Everton who was out there. The French coppers had him in custody for extradition back to England. He picked up more than a druggie while he was out there, I'll tell you. I keep asking myself, what the hell is a babe like Pascale doing with my dad?'

'Why? What's up with your dad?'

'He's going bald, he's ugly, he smokes forty a day and he's not even rich or anything. Even the music he likes is crap – *opera* for God's sake!'

'He must have something going for him, Daniel. This Pascale must see something in him.'

'Well I certainly can't see why she's so happy to be with him, Luke.'

'To you, he's Dad, to her though . . . it's hard to tell what goes on between a man and a woman. But she sounds like a real doll.'

'She is a doll, but that's not what Mum calls her.'

'What does your mum call her?'

'Frog, slag . . . French tart, bitch, prostitute, sleaze ball, tramp, home wrecker, cow, scumbag . . . foreign item, whore-features, trashy bint. It depends how mad she's feeling at the time. It depends on how much she's been drinking. Often the two go hand in hand.'

'So they're not being grown-up and mature about it all!'

'No.'

'What's your mum look like?'

'The opposite of Pascale. Short, unremarkable, a woman, dyes her hair black . . .'

'Sounds like it was all a bit harsh on your mum.'

I couldn't believe what I'd just heard; I laughed sourly and shook my head.

'No. Oh no, no, no! No, Luke. Just . . . hang on, that's exactly the sort of thing she'd want to hear, the sort of thing she wants people to say. For two years she's been going around acting all injured and wanting people to feel sorry for her. The big wronged woman. At home, she's either sitting around and saying nothing or ranting on about them and blowing her top over nothing. I don't know what I'm coming home to most nights. Sad or mad or both? But, do you know something, Luke, I reached a stage where I stopped caring what I came home to because I just got bored. The act just got too hard to swallow. So when I was invited over to Paris . . .'

'When was this?'

'Last summer. I went and stayed with them for a week. It was brilliant. They laugh a lot. They talk instead of shout at mealtimes. They go out places!'

I stopped and drew breath, suddenly feeling hot and unwell but also feeling I had to go on, I had to tell it all how it was, even the really big secret at the heart of my parents' situation, the secret I'd sworn to Mum I'd take to my deathbed.

'Your mum has had a raw deal, Daniel, and, yeah, maybe she has taken it hard. But you can't blame her.'

'Listen, Luke, I'm going to tell you a secret about my mum. She's had an affair herself. I don't know who he was but he looked a lot like Bruce Springsteen!'

Luke burst out laughing. 'Bruce Springsteen?' He could see I was annoyed at his outburst, apologised and quietened down.

'Three years ago, I came home early from school and caught them. God, it was horrible, like a nightmare. They didn't hear me coming into the house. They were in the bathroom! She made me swear not to tell anyone.

So I didn't, I haven't, until now. I didn't tell Dad even. You're the only person I've told, Luke.' The old sense of rising nausea came back to me as I recalled opening the bathroom door. It had taken me some months to erase the sharper details of that afternoon, but the overwhelming shock of it all was still capable of sneaking up and giving me a full headbutt. 'So, no,' I carried on, 'when Mum starts on about Dad and Pascale, and what they are and what they aren't, I don't really have any sympathy . . .' There was a deep silence in the tent and I was feeling less and less able to carry on. I suddenly craved dreamless sleep and healing calm for my pounding head.

'So why head for London?' asked Luke. 'Why didn't you go to Paris?'

'Because they're happy enough without me. They don't need me. I'd only wreck their happiness.'

There was an embarrassed silence, made sharper by the confined space and broken only when Luke said, 'From what you've said, I'm surprised your mother allowed you to go to Paris on holiday, Daniel.'

'She had no choice in the matter.'

'How do you mean?' asked Luke.

'Well, if she didn't let me go, I threatened to tell everyone about her little *oh là là!* with Bruce Springsteen.'

'I see why you left home,' he said, as he lay down and turned out the torch. 'Night, Daniel!'

I listened to the rustle of nylon as he turned over in his sleeping bag and nuzzled down as best he could on the hard ground. I wondered if I'd done the right thing in telling the secret. It didn't matter, I told myself, none of it mattered any more. I lay down, the flesh along my spine puckering into a hundred thousand electric goose bumps as a single drop of sour sweat ran the length of my aching backbone.

7

The Fire

I dreamed of fire, a field of swaying corn catching alight on a brilliant summer's day, a wave of flames, leaping to the picture book blue sky as it raced across the ground, consuming all it touched. The wave of fire grew stronger and quicker with each moment as it fed on the corn and raced towards me in fast forward. I was stuck, dead centre in the cornfield, tied to a post in the ground and dressed in rags. The first of the flames to reach me licked at the loose straw that hung from the hem of my tattered trousers, while overhead a glistening, jet black raven wheeled around the sky, cackling at me, 'Scarecrow! Scarecrow!' I screamed, but made no sound, my mouth fixed and set, my screams a mere silence in a straw man's heart.

I dreamed I was nothing more than a burning effigy swathed in choking, dense black smoke . . .

Smoke . . . Smoke drifted into the tent with the first light of morning through the unzipped entrance.

'Luke?' I could barely speak and, during a few hours of troubled sleep, the virus had taken full possession of my being. Smoke curled and twisted into my burned-out throat and I coughed grim graveyard bursts as I crawled for the entrance. Luke's sleeping bag formed a shapeless heap in the corner and I was suddenly scared of what I was going to see outside, but the fear of being trapped in a burning tent sent my weak body scuttling into the morning sunshine.

The source of the bitter smoke was a fire, a small fire just between the tent and the Range Rover. Luke was crouched over the campfire, poking at it with a bent stick and sending wreaths of smoke from its smouldering heart. I covered my mouth and nose as the pillar of smoke drifted past me and stayed at a safe distance, watching.

'How are you feeling?' he asked. I made no reply; he turned and looked back at me. 'You look awful, Daniel, but never mind, eh, we'll soon have you tucked up safe and sound before . . .' His attention drifted back to the fire which he watched with faraway eyes.

I hobbled barefoot over the uneven ground and stood over him, wondering what it was he was burning. I'd lost my sense of smell but the smoke was dense and dark and deeply unpleasant in texture. It looked like he was burning a heavy blanket but, whatever it was, it was so charred it was impossible to tell what it had been. He had a metal petrol can in one hand which he banged on the ground, like a soft, steady beat from a hollow tin drum. It looked as if he was praying.

'What are you burning?' I croaked. He stared into the remains of the fire, not looking at me once as he spoke. 'Remember when we were in the hotel, when we were at table, waiting to eat, and we had that conversation about meat. I kind of read your mind, Daniel, at least, I noticed the way you looked at my leather jacket while I was giving my sermon on the evils of meat eating.

There I was condemning eating the cow's flesh while I was sitting in her skin. You put me to shame, Daniel!'

Ah, come on, I thought, nobody's one hundred per cent about anything! But I kept my silence.

'You were right, of course. You didn't speak the word but I've been a hypocrite, a complete hypocrite, not eating meat but going around in an expensive leather jacket. So, that's what I'm burning, my jacket, my £300 leather jacket, the skin of some poor slaughtered animal.'

Maybe he had been saying his prayers, maybe he was at a cremation, I thought. As he rose to his full height and stood beside me, I looked closely at him and was impressed by how sensitive and kind he looked. He continued to stare into the blubbering flame holding the petrol can to his heart like he was nursing a baby.

'I've been the most . . . stupid hypocrite and I want to thank you, Daniel, for showing me that I've been wrong. I've done both of us a big favour this morning. I've burned my leather and your suede jacket.'

'Christ!' I uttered the word quietly and I don't know whether he heard me or not but he certainly didn't make any attempt to reply. My suede jacket, my beautiful suede jacket that I'd worked so hard for, for so long, in the wind and the cold and the rain, all those early mornings, the crazed dogs and narked pensioners, and all it was now was a mass of ashes and dust, cinders and lifeless soot. The last time I'd seen it was when I threw it on the back seat next to his leather.

He was smiling at me – I could tell from the corner of my eye – but I couldn't bring myself to look at him.

It was like identifying the mutilated corpse of a once beautiful and much loved friend.

'Daniel, it was the right thing to do, for both of us. And I know you loved wearing that suede jacket, believe me, I loved wearing that leather, but, sometimes you just have to be bigger than what you want.'

He faced me directly, he more or less thrust his face into mine, he made me look at him and nothing else.

'That fox had a skin, the one we saw hunted down and slaughtered, she had a skin. People used to think it was all right to wear fox fur! What's the difference between that fox and the cow who had her skin taken?'

With great difficulty, I spoke. 'You could've asked me first.'

'You were asleep.'

'Why didn't you wake me?'

'You aren't well.'

'Well, you should've woken me.'

'I had to seize the moment. It was hard for me, you know. This is as much a sacrifice for me as it is for you. More even. I was the one who lit the fire. It had to be done, Daniel. If . . . if I hadn't done it now, maybe I wouldn't have found the strength to do it some other time. Then we'd have both been walking round covered in the skin of the dead.'

His eyes drilled into mine, searching out the throbbing core of my brain, urging me to see it the only way it could be seen, his way. Below, the fire was going out and it occurred to me that all I'd lost was a jacket, a single piece of clothing, not an arm or a leg, not my life or freedom . . . which is exactly what some cow had lost to provide it, just like the fox yesterday had lost her life for the amusement of the hunters. And what choice did they have in the matter? If I'd continued to wear the suede jacket, then what would the difference have been between me and the hunters?

'I guess,' I said, 'you did the right thing.'

'Yes, I did, didn't I?'

He lightened up immediately and clapped his hands on my shoulders. He laughed, his eyes twinkling. 'We'd have been as bad as the redcoats if we'd carried on walking about in leather and suede.'

'I just thought that, kind of.'

'Great minds think alike, Daniel! You've been a hypocrite too, but it's all right now.'

My head felt like it was spinning around like a special effect on a video game, about to explode.

'We'll get everything packed up and get you to a hotel. The sooner the better.'

He left the cremation and headed back for the tent which he set about packing up with swift and sure movements. I stole a glance at the ashes and remembered the way it fitted me so well and how it creased at the elbow. I recalled how warm it was when I turned the collar up and when I zipped and buttoned it down the front I felt bullet-proof and cool.

Thin smoke stung my eyes and scratched the back of my throat. I wanted to get my trainers and get away from the field. I followed him to the tent which was now folded and bundled in his arms.

He smiled very sweetly and said, 'Come on, let's get you sorted out, Daniel!'

I sat on the damp, dewy grass to get my trainers on.

He should have asked me first. He really should have done.

8

Healthy Living

'What time is it?' I opened my eyes and focused on the ceiling above my head. In the air-conditioned comfort of our hotel room, with its smoked glass window, it was impossible to tell if it was day or night. I raised my head and looked down the length of my bed. Luke was sitting on a chair at the foot of the bed, as he had been every time I woke up, reading a book. 'Luke, what's the time?' My voice was clearer, stronger. He placed his book down and smiled, 'Back in the land of the living, are we?'

I felt washed out, like I'd been hung, drawn and quartered and stitched together again with knitting needles and secondhand string, but I was feeling much, much better.

'You've been in and out of sleep for two days and nights.'

'What time is it?'

'Getting on for midnight. Friday midnight!'

I'd lost forty-eight hours of my life. In the brief spells I had woken, it was to Luke giving me sips of ice-cold water and wiping my face and head down with wet flannels. I'd had hallucinations in which the walls of the room seemed to be breathing and the ceiling rolling back and forth like gentle ocean waves, with only Luke's voice to calm me.

'You've had a really bad attack, Daniel. You're going to have to take it easy getting better. We'll stick round here for a few more days.'

'But what about the money?'

'Don't worry about money. Are you hungry?'

I was very hungry indeed. Luke picked up the phone and ten minutes later there was a knock at the door. It was room service with vegetable soup and bread rolls.

He sat beside me on the bed as I lifted a spoonful of soup. I was shaking and spilled the soup on the tray as I tried to raise it to my lips. He took the spoon from me and slowly and carefully spooned soup to my lips; he stopped and broke bread into the bowl. 'Take it easy,' he urged me, as he patiently fed me. I had to hand it to him, I hadn't been cared for like this since an attack of measles when I was in the Infants. I became consumed by a raging thirst and, without a word, he went to the mini-bar and came back with a bottle of still mineral water which he poured into a glass. He steadied his hand around mine as I drank and told me, 'Sip the water, Daniel, don't drink it too quickly. Sip it nice and slowly.' He fixed the pillow behind me and I sank back, exhausted.

'Thanks, thanks, Luke,' I said. My eyes drifted to the phone by the bedside; it occurred to me I should phone home and tell her I was feeling better. But as thoughts went, it was an uninvited and most unwanted guest and so I ignored it, hoping it would get the message and leave quietly. But it didn't, it lingered.

'There's no point,' I mumbled to myself.

'There's no point to what?' my friend asked.

'Phoning home to tell Mum I'm better. She doesn't even know I'm ill in the first place . . . What's that you're reading?' I asked, changing the subject fast.

He showed me the cover, a happy family and the title, *The Illustrated Family Medical Encyclopaedia*. He was looking away, like he wouldn't look straight at me and I felt strangely unsettled. 'What's wrong, Luke?' I asked.

'Don't get upset, Daniel, you won't get upset, will you?'

'I don't know. Why? What is it could upset me?'

'Don't go mad . . .'

'Don't go mad,' I echoed his words, panic stalking me like a ten-legged beast.

'Look, Daniel, I won't beat about the bush.' I was convinced he was about to toss a bombshell into my lap.

'What've you done, Luke? What's wrong?'

'Nothing's wrong. Hear me out. Please.' Luke indicated the telephone with a quick hand gesture. 'I called your mother. I told her you were OK!'

'Why?' I pushed the tray away slightly. Without a further word, Luke carried it away for me. 'I told her you were safe and . . . well, quite well in yourself.'

'Why, Luke?' He placed the tray down and leaned on the edge of a wide desk in the corner of the room. He folded his arms and said nothing.

'So, what did she say?' I tried to sound neutral and uninterested. For a moment I heard Luke humming that tune, again, in the back of his throat, as if he wasn't really listening to me. 'Did she say anything?' I tried again.

'She asked if you'd come home. I told her that was your decision.'

'Did she ask who you were?'

'A friend, I told her.'

'Yeah, well there's no way I'm going back home. No way on earth. Did she say anything else?'

'Yes.'

'What did she say, Luke?'

'She said if you went home, you could sit down and talk things through. She said that whatever was wrong, it wasn't impossible to get over. She said she'd try and make things right, that things would be different. She said she was sorry if she'd done anything to drive you away. She said she hoped you were well. She said she loves you and that if you came home, she'd make sure there were no problems with school. She told me to tell you . . . don't do anything that's dangerous or going to harm you. She sounded nice. She was crying.'

This was a side to Mum I'd almost forgotten existed, it'd been such a long time since I'd heard her talk like that. Crying? Maybe the conniving cow was just trying to get Luke onto her side.

'Well, why didn't she say any of those things when I was stuck at home getting bollocked at the drop of a hat just because she was in a permanent nark?'

'I'm just passing on her messages, Daniel.'

'You shouldn't have called in the first place. It was stupid of you!'

'Oh, but I had to!' His voice cracked like a whip and his whole face darkened. He was holding onto the edge of the desk, as if trying to keep himself from doing something destructive with his hands. '*Stupid*? Don't you ever talk to me like that! D'you understand?'

'I'm sorry, Luke, I didn't mean it!' I wasn't lying or apologising lightly. He took a deep breath and we sat in silence as he calmed down until I opened my mouth to speak but he held a hand up to silence me.

'I had to phone your home, Daniel. I needed to know if you took medication.'

'Medication?'

'Yeah, medication. I was scared, you see. I didn't know what to do. The thing is, you had a fit yesterday afternoon.'

His eyes searched out mine as he sat at the bottom of the bed and the look on his face left me in no doubt that he was telling the truth. I had a deep sinking feeling, like the afternoon I got home from school and Dad's things were gone, mixed up with the time I got caught shoplifting in HMV but, somehow, worse.

'But I've never had a fit in my life. People in our family don't have fits.'

I was feeling worse by the second. Fits? Fits were for mental patients and the sad oddities who spent their lives in public parks talking to imaginary animals. Surely, I just wasn't the type to have a fit.

'I saw a woman on a bus having a fit, people didn't know what to do. They didn't know whether to look at her or look out of the window. This bloke sat next to her on the floor and put her head on his lap when it was all over; she'd cracked her head on the front of the seat. There's no epileptics in our family.'

'I know. Your mum told me. Your mum got a bit freaked out when I asked if you had epilepsy. I told her not to worry, all you had was a bad dose of 'flu.'

'She will worry, she worries about everything, she worries if she isn't worried. What happened, when I . . .?'

'When you had the fit? Yesterday afternoon, you were just in bed and, it was like you were waking up and . . .' He clicked his fingers. 'You went out like a light, arms and legs jerking about, foaming at the mouth a bit.'

I covered my face with my hands. 'You're overreacting, Daniel. Epilepsy can be dealt with. It doesn't mean you're a mental case, there are half a million epileptics in Britain and . . . It might've been a one-off caused by stress . . .'

What was next? I wondered. What evil thing lay waiting? 'Luke! Luke, you won't tell anyone, will you?'

'Of course I won't. But you're going to have to visit a doctor. It can be kept in line with drugs, you know. If you are an epileptic. Soon as you're up and about. You'll get yourself checked out. Promise me?'

'I will, yes, I will!'

He handed me the medical book, open at the E section, on the page that dealt with epilepsy. I'd already read it, in the local library back home, so often in fact that I could almost tell it back word for word, off by heart. After I'd seen the woman fitting on the bus, I'd checked back as far as I could in the family. How relieved

I'd been, how downright pleased when I could find no sign of it.

'Daniel, you've nothing to fear or be ashamed of.' Though it was easy for him to be big about it.

'I know that but you won't tell anyone, will you, Luke?'

★   ★   ★

Luke was tiptoeing out of the room, opening the door so so quietly, when I sprang awake from the lightest of sleeps.

'Where are you going?' I sat up in bed.

'I'm going to sell the Range Rover.'

'Eh?' I heard him perfectly clearly but I couldn't believe it.

'I've run out of money. The room costs a hundred a day, not including food.'

'We wouldn't be here if it wasn't for me!' I said, looking around the room. 'No, hang on, Luke. Is there anything I can do to . . .?'

'Rob a building society!' he laughed. 'Look, don't worry about it. It was a mad vehicle to buy. It cleaned me out of all my compo money. I really ought to get something more economical.'

'Luke . . . what did you get compensation for?'

'The Criminal Injuries Board.' His body language told me he was eager to be out of the room. 'The sooner I do it, the sooner we're in the money. See you later, Daniel.'

As soon as he was gone, my thoughts went straight back home to Liverpool. I'd have loved to have listened in on the call he'd made to Mum. So, she wanted me to go home and work it all out, did she? This was the same woman who, just over a week ago, told me, without a glimmer of a smile, 'If I had the money, Danny, I'd buy you a one-way ticket to Australia. Who knows, maybe I could pay the airline by instalments?' The bitter truth, I knew in my heart: I was a living, breathing disappointment to her.

I looked at the telephone and, without thinking about it, found the receiver in my hand, pressed close to my face while I dialled the 0151 area code for Liverpool. I stopped – what would I say? Whatever happened, I wasn't going back. Ever. I dialled 428, after all there was no need for me to dial the rest. The thing was, she mightn't even be at home. I dialled three more digits, my index finger hovering over the final 8.

Even if there was a reply, I didn't have to speak, just as long as I could hear her voice and know that she was all right. I don't know what made me think of it but the place she worked, the restaurant by the Pier Head, it got dark round there at nights, dark and dangerous . . .

The ringing tone sounded, an amplified heartbeat passed through a sound distortion chamber. It rang out fully once, I counted, and before the second one could chime, the receiver at the other end was snatched up. 'Hello, hello . . .' It was her. She sounded tired and a little shaky, but not exactly demented with worry. 'Danny, is that you? Danny, just let me know if that's you, let me know you're all right. Please.'

Slowly, I replaced the receiver, abandoning it to the hook, closing the line of communication. I didn't wish her any harm, I wished her well, but there was just too much bad blood between us. I watched the still and silent receiver and whispered, 'Yes, it's me. I'm fine. Thank you.'

★   ★   ★

The hotel room had an en suite bathroom and a large screen television set. Since I'd left home, I'd almost forgotten they existed so when I switched on the TV it was like opening a door and seeing the smiling face of a long lost friend. 'Sesame Street'. I flicked around the channels, soaps, chat shows, old films, satellite news . . . nothing for me really so I turned back into the closing credits of 'Sesame Street' and went through to run a bath. It was like a bathroom in a movie, spotless, everything laid out – soaps, gels, powders and fat, fluffy towels – everything matching, chrome taps that sparkled and a gleaming white bathtub, a perfect room in fact.

I caught sight of my reflection in the large square mirror on the wall above the bath. *This is just a dream . . . this is not a dream . . .* it was a sound bite from the TV next door piped into the bathroom through a pair of built-in speakers. I looked in the mirror. It was not a pretty sight. My hair was matted where I'd slept on it and my forehead was marked by a band of wild acne.

My eyes were lost in valleys of darkness. I'd been plain-looking. Now I was plain and rough-looking. And I'd had a fit.

I sat on the edge of the bath to get out of the mirror's glare and turned on the taps, drowning out the sound of the TV. It started hitting home, I was now a person who had fits, maybe I'd soon be a person who had fits in front of other people, maybe on the bus, or while being served at the counter at McDonald's, perhaps walking into crowded rooms of people falling into embarrassed silence while I thrashed and writhed on the middle of the carpet.

I looked over my shoulder and there was a news broadcast on TV, local news headlines, I couldn't hear the words, but I could see the newscaster, her mouth moving as she read from the autocue. Boring.

I found a tube of bath foam and squeezed the sweet smelling jelly into the swirling water, a thick foam rose where the water cascaded into the tub. I looked in the mirror and saw on TV an image that made the blood drain from my head, hands and feet.

It was Bowler Hat's face.

I turned off the taps as quickly as I could, glancing in the mirror as I did so, as Bowler Hat seemed to stare straight back into my eyes. The water swayed and eddied and the newscaster's voice slipped out of the speakers.

'George Parkinson is still in a coma. The police are waiting at his bedside to question him and still wish to interview two youths in connection with the attack.'

I stepped quickly into the bath, the water almost un-bearably hot and scrubbed each piece of skin I could reach with the complimentary brush and soap, scraping and boiling my body clean of the crime.

Bowler Hat – real name, then, George Parkinson – Parkinson's face vanished from the TV screen but his eyes seemed to linger on, reflected in the bathroom mirror, caught in the gleaming chrome of the taps, looking directly at me, staring at me, accusing me!

As Luke returned to the room, smiling past himself, I climbed out of the tub.

'Get in here, Daniel, I've got some news for you.' Soaking wet and wrapped in towels, I appeared in the bathroom doorway.

Luke threw down a new set of car keys onto his bed and a fat envelope of bank notes. He rubbed his hands together and smiled at me.

'What's wrong, Daniel?'

'I've got some news as well,' I said. 'You'd better prepare yourself for a shock, Luke.'

9

Back on the Road Again

Luke knew all about Bowler Hat being in a coma. He'd seen it on the news while I'd been out for the count. As I told him what I'd seen, and fear reached boiling point inside my head, he listened with a passive grin on his face. 'If the guy dies, it's called manslaughter,' I said.

'Manslaughter,' he chuckled.

'What's funny about that? Could you please enlighten me?'

'There's nothing funny about manslaughter. It's just you, panicking like an old woman and dressed like one of those Roman Emperors. Now that's funny.'

'They're looking for two youths.'

'That narrows it down to a few hundred thousand I guess.'

'What if someone saw us? Someone must've seen us.' I spoke my thoughts out loud, the words bouncing off the walls and smacking me about the face and head, as Luke stifled a long slow yawn.

'No one saw us.'

'How can you be so sure?'

'It was dark, there was no one on the street and the whole thing lasted about twenty seconds.'

'It didn't feel like twenty seconds, it seemed to last

for . . .' I didn't know. It felt like a slow hour on one hand, a fast fifteen seconds on the other.

'See what I mean, Daniel. You were bang there in the middle of it all and you aren't sure of the facts. The cops couldn't make anything stick. Trust me. If, and it's a colossal *if*, we did get collared for it, I'll take entire responsibility; I'll tell it the way it was. It was a bit of a prank that got out of hand, you were in the dark about it. I'll take the flak!'

In saying this, he wasn't giving me anything but I found I felt strangely indebted to him and was more than a little horrified to hear myself saying, 'I was there as well, you know. I do have some part in this mess.'

'He was pissed, he fell over and banged his head,' Luke said, chucking me the fat bundle of bank notes. 'There's no problem!' He was wrong, of course.

There was a problem; but it was a shared one.

'How much?' I asked, flicking through the bundle of bank notes.

'Twelve thousand,' he said. *Twelve thousand? On a nearly brand new Range Rover that must've cost something over twenty?* He'd been robbed.

He jangled a shabby set of keys. 'And an old red Escort.' He'd still been conned soft but I didn't feel in a position to pass comment. 'A red Escort?' I said, remembering. 'Just like Dad used to drive.' Years ago, the first car I ever remember travelling in, strapped into a seat in the back, while Mum and Dad laughed and joked and sweet talked up front. The past was a very weird place sometimes. I stepped out of the towels and started pulling on my boxers.

'I want to get going, Luke.'

'Are you up to it?'

'I'm up to it,' I said. Though it was not so much a case of being up to it as a case of not being up to hanging around and getting caught.

★ ★ ★

The hotel had an underground car park where the V–reg Escort was parked away from the other cars in an enclave of shadows, cast where the artificial ceiling lights kissed the concrete pillars that held up the low ceiling. As we walked towards the car, our footsteps echoed around the bare walls giving an illusion that the car park was stalked by a tribe of invisible men. I was spooked by the notion and clutched the money, wrapped in a carrier bag, and looked around, half expecting some real life mugger to leap out and snatch the cash. I'd never seen so much cash in my life, never mind had it in my hands. It was a strange thing but when I'd lost everything in the service station I felt safer than I did walking along with all that money.

'What are we going to do?' I asked.

'About?' Luke sighed.

'The money. Are you going to pay it into a bank?'

He stopped, laughed and asked, 'Do I look like a black man to you?'

'Pardon?' I was shocked.

75

'I'm eighteen years old, Daniel,' Luke informed me. 'So I walk into the Nat West on the high street and open an account with twelve grand. They'd have the drug squad down there before we hit the pavement. Yo' understand, homeboy? That's the act of a not very bright black drug dealer. Like I said, do I look like a black man to you? Do I?'

'I just – I don't . . .' I couldn't believe what he'd said. Sure, I'd heard this sort of talk a thousand times from some knuckleheads I'd been unlucky enough to be schooled with, but coming from him it sounded alien, like he'd been taken over by the spirit of some skid row demon with an ultra low IQ.

I decided not to pursue the matter, to shut up and let it drop. No one was perfect, I told myself. He smiled in my face. There's something wrong with everyone and this was his thing. He rabbit punched the bag of money that I nursed into my chest and said, 'Let's sort out the lolly!'

He opened the car up and produced a set of screwdrivers from the glove compartment. As I climbed into the passenger side, he started taking the black vinyl side panel from the driver's door.

'What are you doing?' I asked.

'This is our bank,' he replied. 'We'll stash the money in here.' He pulled the panel away to reveal a deep, gaping hiding place. 'Good, eh?' He winked at me. Good? It was a terrible idea. If the car got stolen, then the money went with it. But it was his car and his money and who was I to argue? I couldn't even hold onto a Nike sports bag.

★   ★   ★

The Escort was very much like the one I'd learned to drive in, fairly rust-free, with seats like battered armchairs, the kind of car you wouldn't look at twice and just the sort of vehicle we needed in our situation.

It even had a radio which had fairly clear reception on which we listened to a rock music station. I tried forgetting our problems, and didn't notice the sudden passage of time, as I gazed through the window, fast retreating into myself, recalling the words of old songs and saying them quietly in my head.

Out of the silence between us, he spoke calmly. 'I don't believe it.'

It was like a voice from beyond, to which I echoed, 'What?'

He slowed down onto the hard shoulder and pulled up. He reached into the back of the car and opened the AA Road Atlas. He found the page he wanted. I glanced at his lap and, as I always did when confronted with maps, felt myself come over all dyslexic.

'Where did we go wrong? Well, would you believe it?'

'Believe what?'

'When we left the hotel in Oxford, I thought we'd head south . . . how did I? I thought it looked a bit familiar. We're heading north, back Banbury way.'

'Banbury way, Banbury as in on the way to Dunvegan Hall?'

'Don't panic. We're not really very near it at the moment.'

It was a genuine but horrendous mistake. Could I really feel my heart clenching and the blood streaming through the veins and arteries? 'I need the toilet,' I announced.

'There's a service station, a couple of miles up the road, we'll get a coffee while we're there. Sorry about this,' he said, as we hit the motorway.

'It's not your fault,' I replied, my stomach knotting and untying, a riot of sharpening pain and anxiety as we headed back towards the crime scene.

10

Girls

I splashed cold water on my face and as the colour came back to my cheeks, I felt that this attack of the runs was a one-off.

The service station café was just like the one where we'd met, only a lot busier and I couldn't see where he was sitting. A sudden peal of laughter rose from the soundscape, and then a blanket of giggling. I walked slowly, looking around without trying to be seen. There was the laughter again that stood out from the crowd like a lunatic on stilts. It was a group of girls by the sound of it and it came from round the corner. I followed the noise and found him at a table in the corner facing three girls, a blonde, a redhead and a dark-haired girl, their backs to me so I couldn't see their faces. I could tell they were hooked by Luke as he pulled levers in their minds and made them giggle and laugh. He shot a look past them and caught my eye. 'Daniel, hey, I thought you got lost!'

As I sat down next to Luke I had my first look at the three girls whose attention was fixed on him. I looked again. And again. And again at the dark-haired girl opposite me and choked back the urge to blurt, 'I don't believe this!' I dragged my eyes away from her but found them drawn back irresistibly. It was Kathy, not in a hunting coat and black hat this time but a blue designer jacket.

Slowly, she turned to me, buckled at my uninvited attention and asked, 'What are you looking at?'

'Your jacket. It's great.'

'By the way,' Luke changed the subject, 'this is Daniel. Daniel, this is Kathy.' He indicated the blonde. 'And Laura!' And then the redhead. 'Last but not least, Jayne!'

'I was thinking, I've seen you before,' I said to Kathy. 'I was trying to picture where that was!'

'Bad chat-up line!' Jayne groaned.

'I don't think so,' said Kathy. 'I don't think I've ever seen you before.'

'Then it's a case of mistaken identity. I'm sorry.'

'We're not from round here,' commented Luke. 'But, yes, I can see what you mean, Daniel. You do have a familiar look, Kathy!' There was something in the way he spoke that made me go thoroughly cold and unnaturally hot.

Luke turned to me with a conspiratorial smile and asked, 'Did you get the batteries for the camera OK?'

I was glad he didn't ask how my diarrhoea was, and so happily lied, 'Yeah, I got the batteries. No problem, Luke.'

Laura and Jayne started giggling, at first quietly into each other's faces and then directly at me. When Laura calmed down enough she asked, 'Are you from Ireland or somewhere like that?'

'He's not Irish, he's a Scouser, dimwit!' Jayne now laughed at Laura, too loudly and, now, people at the tables around us were turning their heads and looking over with a mixture of curiosity and irritation. Kathy clapped a hand on Jayne's shoulder, 'Calm down, for God's sake!'

I caught Kathy's eye, as I looked over the rim of my coffee cup. 'Are you their care assistant?' Jayne and Laura's faces fell, realising it was their turn to be the target of a joke.

'It feels like that sometimes, yeah,' she agreed.

'So, where are you heading?' asked Luke. They looked at each other uncertainly for a moment; Jayne and Laura made a show of looking even more vacant than nature had made them.

'It's a secret,' I announced, as Luke drew Kathy in with a smile.

'You don't have to tell if you don't want to,' he whispered to her. He then looked at his watch and moved his chair back, making it clear he was prepared to leave. Wherever they were going it was going to be fun and somewhere they weren't supposed to be. And wherever it was, whatever they were doing, they didn't want us along with them.

'We don't really know you,' said Kathy. *That's right! I thought. But we know a load about you.* 'It's nothing personal,' she went on, 'but . . .'

'Well, where are you going?' asked Laura, suddenly, with a head flick that could have caused whiplash to someone less practised in the art.

'Us? We're making a film!' said Luke.

'Liar!' Jayne declared.

'We're making a documentary film. Luke's directing, I work the camera.'

Three faces; Laura believed us, Jayne wasn't sure and Kathy appeared completely unbothered.

Ten minutes later, they were standing by the boot of the Escort, looking down at the box of videotapes. I slipped a tape into the camcorder and panned the camera across their faces. Jayne and Laura got the giggles while Kathy walked off camera, embarrassed. 'Turn it off!'

Laura asked, 'What do we do? What do you want us to do?'

'Come back, Kathy!' called Jayne. 'Come on, the film's about *all* of us.' Their uncertainty was rapidly cooling off.

'I'm not sure, I hate being filmed,' Kathy complained, as she watched and her ego warmed up a little. As she drifted back to her friends, Luke touched my arm, wanting my attention.

I turned the camera off and looked at him. I could tell. For once, he didn't know quite what to do with them. 'Get them to walk towards camera, telling us something about themselves!'

He lined them up at a short distance and – it was amazing how obedient they became for the camera – they walked towards me like a six-legged, three-headed beast, speaking from left to right.

'My name's Kathy, I'm seventeen . . . and I'm finding this highly embarrassing.'

'I'm Jayne, I'm seventeen too, I'm from Cheltenham,

we all are, my dad makes tractors, well he owns a factory that makes tractors . . . I'm going to be a star!'

'I'm Laura, I'm sixteen, this is brilliant, I'm going to Drama school soon, our parents think we're visiting some friends but we're hitching to a rave, an all-nighter, the DJ's Stevie Allen and he's got a mobile rig!'

I kept the camera on Laura's face while Kathy and Jayne turned on her. 'Shut up, motor mouth!' said Jayne, as Kathy mimed zipping her mouth. Her great big mouth, her fat face – their words – fell suddenly silent. How young Laura looked under attack from her friends, her face a puddle of sulks and a picture of hurt feelings.

Luke grinned and whispered, 'And guess who they're taking with them, Daniel?'

As we drove away from Banbury, their only snatch of conversation – hushed and hurried so that we couldn't hear, which we could, of course – for the first half hour went like this.

'Why can't you keep anything to yourself, Laura?' Happy Jayne sounded like a different kettle of fish now. 'You're just . . . you can't be trusted.'

'It just came out, OK!'

I couldn't look at Luke, for fear of laughing.

'You don't mind us coming along, do you?' chimed Luke, brightly.

'Not at all,' lied Kathy. 'Laura, why don't you think before you open your mouth?' She was obviously thinking very hard about this one but she didn't reply.

As we drove on into early evening, the motorway road

signs told us we were getting closer and closer to Chipping Norton.

'How'd you get to hear about it?' I asked.

'It was a pirate radio station, Radio Doom, they're throwing up a marquee!' Kathy replied. 'They said only tell your friends, don't bring people you don't know.'

'People like us?' I spoke her mind for her. 'We're not trouble. We're dead peace-loving, aren't we, Luke?'

'Wouldn't hurt a fly, Daniel.'

'It's just that we hardly know you,' Jayne announced.

'It's fair enough,' Luke spoke. 'So why don't you give us the directions, we drive you there and then we say *adios, amigos!* Then you're not with us if we decide to murder any innocent bystanders.' Their mood lightened immediately. They had the best of both worlds, a ride there and us off their backs. Luke went on, 'But I'm going to need slightly more detailed directions than a marquee in a field somewhere outside Chipping Norton!' He eyed Kathy through the rear view mirror. She reached into her pocket and handed a piece of folded A4 paper to me which I immediately opened out. It was a list of instructions, names of A roads and turn-offs with a carefully hand-drawn map.

'We'll get a coffee,' I said to Luke, 'and talk about how we're going to get there. If you don't mind me asking though, how did you think you were going to make it there without a direct lift?'

'It's the first time we've been to one of these things,' Kathy told us.

'Then you're lucky you met us, aren't you!' said Luke, taking the map.

★ ★ ★

We sat at a window table in a Little Chef, hunched over the home-made map and comparing it with the AA Road Atlas. I observed Jayne and Laura as they watched Luke, jotting down a few notes as he worked out the route for the rest of the journey. I found myself touching the edges of my face and wondering why it was that some people were blessed with the sort of looks that drew the gazes of sheer admiration and why, on the other hand, there was my sort? He eyed the map and looked intelligent, I eyed it and looked puzzled; he smiled and looked kind and appealing, I smiled and looked like a bad seaside comedian. Kathy and Laura looked at each other and it was clear they both fancied him. 'No problem!' said Luke, shutting the atlas.

I wondered, sourly, if they'd find him so attractive if they could see him in action with a baseball bat. As soon as this thought formed in my mind, Luke looked directly at me and handed me the map and directions. I avoided his gaze, looking closely at the paper, and shifted out of my seat.

'What's wrong, Daniel?'

'I'm going to the toilet.' I didn't need to go but I was overwhelmed with the urge to get away from Luke and the girls, if only for a couple of minutes. As I got up to go, Kathy emerged from the Ladies, wearing a fresh coat of make-up, and picking up a discarded *Daily Mirror* from an uncleared table. We passed each other with a smile of recognition, a smile that was stillborn on my face when I caught sight of the front page of the newspaper. I turned, said, 'Kathy!'

'Yeah?'

'Can — Can I have a look at the newspaper?' She shrugged and handed it over.

I walked as quickly as I could, without breaking into a run, to the toilet door, praying that my eyes were playing tricks on me, that the picture I'd seen and the headline accompanying it were optical illusions. I clutched the paper in my seeping palm, not daring to look at it under the gaze of other people.

The toilet was empty and I settled uncomfortably on the seat of the nearest cubicle. I took a deep breath, closed my eyes: *Please, please, don't let it be!* I laid the paper down on my lap and, opening my eyes, felt my heart shiver, sending freezing ripples of horror to the crown of my head and the tips of my toes.

The single word headline was BUTCHERED; the victim, his picture underneath the stark news, the blond toddler from Weasel's extended family. Beneath the photograph of the boy were the words, *Kyle . . . slaughtered.*

The door of the room opened and I recognised Luke's footsteps, his voice calling kindly, 'Daniel? Are you all right? Kathy thought you'd seen a ghost or something.' My jaw was locked. I looked at the picture again. Was it definitely him? I read the opening paragraph:

The mutilated body of traveller toddler Kyle Wolf was unearthed by police in a shallow grave in woodland near Banbury.

I was unable to read on. 'Daniel, is the door open? I'm opening the door, OK?'

Luke pushed the door open slowly and crouched down so we were on eye level. My fingers pressed my temples as if trying to stop my skull cracking open and brain leaping out. I was shaking. 'Daniel, what is it?' He looked at the paper and took it from me. 'There are some sick bastards around,' he announced, like he was explaining it away, as if I was a toddler. Luke was inside the cubicle now, closing the door, he clasped my hands in his and looked into my eyes.

'I didn't know they'd found the body,' he said.

'Then you knew, you knew he'd gone missing?'

'It was on the news, on TV.'

'You didn't tell me! Why? We knew that poor kid, not very well, but – Jesus Christ – we knew him!'

'Because I thought you'd be upset. And I was right, wasn't I? You found out and you are upset.'

I couldn't reply, tears were forming in my eyes and I had no will to fight them back. 'His mum'll be destroyed,' I said, as Luke folded the paper and shoved it down the side of the toilet.

'I don't think you should read any more about it, Daniel. It won't do you any good, you know. You'll only be more upset.'

'But I want to know what happened to him!'

Luke clasped my hands again. 'Let's just have a few

moments of quiet respect for poor little Kyle, our little mate.'

I prayed . . . that whoever'd done this died a long, slow, painful death, screaming in agony and despairing of all hope.

'What happened to him?' I broke my hands away and tried to reach the paper. Luke threw his arms around me and spoke softly, 'He was battered to death and he had a knife, with a serrated edge, left in the base of his skull.'

'Why?'

'There are some very sick people out there. What can I say?'

'Was he, was—' It was too awful even to utter.

'Do you mean, was Kyle interfered with? Down below? Sexually? No, thankfully. He was not interfered with. The killer's not like that, according to the news.'

It must have been my imagination, but I could feel a throb where Kyle's foot had connected with my jaw. I held my hand to the spot and grew number and number.

'Do you want to be left alone?' asked Luke. I nodded. He took the newspaper and said, 'Listen, let's not talk about his in front of the girls. OK?'

'Why?'

'What's the point? They'll only go on and on, hoping we can give them a load of stupid details. Let's face it, it's not exactly "University Challenge" out there, is it? What I'm trying to say, Daniel, let's give Kyle some dignity!'

'Yeah, dignity!' I tore some toilet paper from the roll and wiped my face.

'I'll leave you alone then,' said Luke. 'Take your time, get your head together. Wash your face, we'll be waiting for you. OK?'

'OK.'

'Not a word to the girls, eh?'

'Right.'

He patted me on the shoulder and left the room while I stayed exactly where I was, calming myself down and wiping my face. For a long time, I'd wanted to go to an all-night rave but, suddenly, it was the one place I least wanted to be. Perhaps, I thought to myself, if I waited long enough in the toilet, Luke and the girls would forget I was there, or just grow plain impatient and leave without me.

The door of the room opened and Luke said, 'Come on, Daniel, you've been in here half an hour and it's getting a bit awkward out there now!'

'Two minutes!' I replied, and he left. I threw handfuls of water into my face, sweeping my hands across my aching head and flattening my hair down. I looked in the mirror. I looked miserable and angry and confused like a refugee.

Not only had Kyle died a terrible death but the person who'd killed him was out there, walking around and enjoying the sunshine on his ugly, ugly face.

11

Drugs

As night sank down, we became part of a loose convoy of beaten-up cars with enormous stereo systems (easily worth much more than the vehicles themselves), blasting out hardcore dance music.

'What's wrong?' Kathy leaned forward and spoke into the back of my head. I'd almost forgotten they were there and felt suddenly, and painfully, aware of myself. 'You haven't said a word since the Little Chef.'

'I'm all right. Thanks for asking.' Jayne and Laura whispered and started laughing so I turned and said, 'Do you know what the deepest bass sound in the natural world is?' They didn't. I went on. 'The mating cry of the African bull elephant. It took six months to record it because its power screwed up all the recording equipment. You can buy it on CD now but don't turn the volume up too loud or you'll knacker your speakers!'

They looked confused and shut up. Luke kept his finger on the horn and the car in front replied by raising the volume of their sound system.

I raised the camcorder to my shoulder and pointed the lens at the, soon-for-the-scrapyard, Cortina with the four-figure music system. I listened closely to another sound in the near distance. 'Hear that?' I asked. 'That's where we're heading!'

'I can't believe this,' Laura said. 'I've wanted to go to one for years.'

'Mum and Dad don't approve?' replied Luke.

'What do they know?' said Jayne. 'They think everyone just takes a load of drugs and dances till they drop.'

'That's about right, yeah, that's the top and bottom of it!' Luke laughed. 'By the way, while I think on it, I'd take it now, in case there's a search on the door.'

Silence. Kathy asked, 'What do you mean, Luke?'

'What I mean is, I gave Laura and Jayne a couple of Es back in the Chef.'

'They're not doing any drugs,' Kathy said. 'When did he give it to you?'

'He sold it to us,' said Laura, making the distinction between a sale and a gift.

'Look,' Luke spoke over them. He held up a white tablet and dropped it very deliberately into his mouth. His neckline swelled, his adam's apple bulged and pulsed like a snake swallowing a small rodent. 'It's from the same batch. If you buy it in there, you're trusting a stranger . . . it's safe, see.' I tried not to listen as Laura and Jayne continued to bicker in the back with Kathy.

'How are you feeling?' asked Luke.

'I don't want to go to this thing. I might just sit in the car or something.'

'I don't want to sound callous, but there's nothing you can do about the other business. Not now. And moping about certainly isn't going to help.'

'How much did you pay?' Kathy was hitting high decibels now.

'A tenner a tab, you're overreacting!' Laura matched her for volume.

'Did you know about this, Daniel?' Kathy asked, looking for support.

'Kind of . . .' I lied.

'God, am I the only sane one here?' And we fell into a heavy silence.

There was a car ahead of us, a battered up Fiat. I gazed at the back window and hoped I'd see Kyle's face rising up from the darkness. 'What the hell's wrong with this world?' I asked, speaking to myself as much as to Luke.

'The world?' he replied and indicated the whole wide world with the merest, most dismissive flick of the hand. 'This is where we pay for our sins, where we struggle and suffer and die over and over and over again.'

'The drug's taking effect already then,' I said.

'What do you think, Daniel?' Jayne crowed down my ear. 'It's the right of the individual to choose, isn't it?'

'Only if you know what you're choosing. If you don't know what you're choosing, someone else is doing what they want with your brain. If you ask me, that's not freedom of choice, that's being a big time, major dickhead.'

About two minutes later, we were there. It was in a huge marquee in a desolate field in what felt like the middle of nowhere. There were cars and vans parked to one side of the tent but Luke refused to leave the Escort there. 'It's a supermarket for car thieves,' he explained, driving past until we found a sheltered layby at the side of a country lane, near a crossroads.

'Good luck with Spam head and Foo Foo!' I called. Kathy didn't turn or reply. In fact, she walked away like she was heading away from a bad smell.

'What was all that about?' I asked him.

'Aspirin,' he laughed. 'I sold them four aspirin for forty quid.'

'Why?' I asked.

'Call it a fine, a fine on their utter stupidity. Cheer up. Here, take the car keys, mind them like a big boy.'

I could feel the music surging around my body and the beams of light sweeping around me like tides rolling against the darkness. It was like stepping out of the real world and into another place where everything looked, sounded and felt more intense. It was a place where the darkness was pitch and the light was enough to pierce the heart of a stone.

Luke spoke loudly at my side, but I couldn't hear; the music was a blanket that blocked out all other sound.

One of the greatest looking women in the world ran up and down the makeshift stage area where the sound system was set up, calling into her headset microphone for everyone to make more noise and a few hundred whistles rang out piercing the waves of bass beat, sinking back like silver fish flying and falling in a make-believe river. I was eaten alive by the atmosphere and digested by the noise and lights.

Through darkness, I saw the DJ picked out by overhead lights. That was the place to be, up by the sound system; I gripped the camcorder and imagined the type of video I could shoot from the DJ's point of view.

'I'm going up there!' I pointed to myself, the camera, the sound system; Luke seemed to understand and gave me a thumbs up.

He pointed to his watch and showed me five fingers; in case we split up, we'd arranged to meet back at the car at five in the morning.

My head felt weighed down with anguish and loss but I felt something else that proved Luke half right at least. I felt strangely different, numbed by the other world landscape of the gathering. I was talking to myself as I moved past a half-naked girl. Normally, my eyes would've been on stalks but she was just another piece of the action, another curious stitch in the psychedelic fabric.

I pointed the camera and caught the eye of the tall, gangling and bald-headed DJ who looked down at me and waved an arm in my direction. Was he urging me to come closer? Or was that just the way he moved to the music?

There was a long ramp with a bank of amplifiers and loudspeakers powerful enough to cause a dustbowl on the moon, connected to the overhead lighting rig to the rear. I stood and gasped at the machinery that battered the senses and fuelled the sound and vision of this dream world.

The DJ turned and danced; he was moving for the camera and urging me to move closer. As I stepped carefully over the unwound coils of cable, the DJ pointed my attention in the direction of the dance area. I turned the camera on the people and was filled with awe at what I was filming. The crowd was like an imaginary animal, out to play in the manufactured noise and electrical sunlight. It was a big animal with hundreds of heads and thousands of eyes, cloaked by vapour and each of its smaller parts was linked by the electricity that raced around its numerous brains.

Suddenly, the light changed and a battery of strobe lights fell onto the crowd, turning all their manic movements into sharp animations of stark light and staccato darkness. Hands reached up, hands made ghostly by the strobes, hands combined to create the weirdest effect. I thought I could see a collage of Kyle's face, a hundred pictures of him, made out of hands in strobe light, smiling faces, crying faces, his many mouths moving as their fingers writhed, his mouth calling, 'Help me!'

I immediately stopped filming and, shutting my eyes tightly, muttered to myself, 'Go away!' I opened my eyes slowly and the image was gone but I was swamped by the feeling of being completely trapped, and a wild panic soared within me. I could feel my heart banging at my ribs, sweat from my forehead seeping into my eyes and stinging them.

I pictured myself falling, trying to escape but falling, blacking out and having a fit. I saw myself fitting, flailing, frothing at the mouth, falling onto the crowd and being passed over their heads by a conveyor belt of hands.

I clutched the camcorder and hurtled down the ramp as the volume rose higher. I passed a small army of lads, at a rear exit in the marquee, drinking foreign lager and watching the DJ work the crowd, and I ran and ran out into the night.

★ ★ ★

I sat in the driver's seat, absentmindedly turning the key in the ignition and watching the dashboard light up and go out, turn and click, on and off. I turned the key a little harder, a little further, and brought the engine to life. It coughed and rumbled, hummed a steady tone. At least the car was alive.

I looked over my shoulder. There was nothing coming, and I found myself checking the gears in neutral, releasing the handbrake. *Only a little spin, just a few minutes* . . . and I was on the road, pushing twenty mph. The overwhelming sensation of horror, the anxiety, the fear all dissolved away and I was nothing more than a part of the car. There was nothing more than the act of driving down the dark, twisting roads, the death trap bends, the invisible dangers . . . I was doing forty, my knuckles white against the wheel, a film of sweat forming across my forehead. I had no idea where I was going but my sense of me was weakening. I liked the deadness inside me. It was like a drug, taking me away from the shock and misery of the world around me. I was doing fifty-five miles an hour, smiling serenely and feeling good.

In the distance, a pair of headlights swooped around a bend, a car was coming my way and the effect was like a sharp slap in the face. My foot eased back from the accelerator, but the lights were coming at me fast. They obviously hadn't seen me coming in their direction.

The numbness was wearing off fast and my mind was on the blink, not sure what to do for the best because the car coming at me was picking up speed and even though I was down to twenty, there was only one bend between me and it.

There was a narrow embankment on the side of the road, so I turned the wheel sharply and drove up into the hedge as the car screamed past me, probably unaware that it had just avoided a head-on collision.

The engine was still running and the car slid out of the hedge, backwards down the embankment. I was shocked and scared and shaking but unharmed. I carried off down the road and wondered if I had enough petrol to make it back to Liverpool. No, no, no . . . I couldn't go back home, I couldn't leave Luke, I couldn't take his car and his money.

I saw a sign up ahead, a picnic area at the side of the road and headed for it. I turned in and turned the engine off. My head sailed down to the wheel and sleep wrapped itself around me. I'd have a nap and make my way back. After I'd had a sleep. After I'd escaped the waking world, if only for a short time.

12

Blue Light

I overslept. Night hadn't quite gone and day still wasn't here as I drove back down the lanes to where we'd arranged our five o'clock meeting. In the distance, above the line of the hedges, there was a dense haze of flashing blue lights coming right down the road towards me. I froze but carried on and turned swiftly into a grass siding, wide enough to park on, and turned the engine off. As the lights came nearer, without their sirens wailing, I shifted into the passenger seat and waited with gritted teeth. I listened, weaving my damp fingers in and out of each other as the sound of their engines grew louder, I tried to look through them as they took the bend, came into view, came nearer to me.

I reeled off a story to explain myself during that nervous minute which seemed to last an agonising hour; there was a marked police car at the head of the line of vehicles. ('I'm waiting for my friend, Officer!' I rehearsed the line. 'Yes, I know he shouldn't have parked here really. But he was feeling unwell. Rave? What rave, Officer?') I wanted to jump out of the car and hide in the hedges but an invisible weight pressed down on my head keeping me pinned in the passenger seat.

There were two uniformed coppers in the first car. It was followed closely by an ambulance, which was followed by another police car and a motorcycle rider. They switched off the flashing blue lights. I watched them from the corner of my eye, wishing I was a chameleon fading into the background. The ambulance passed me, then the police car and the bike, not seeming to notice me. I waited. And waited some more. I breathed a long, slow sigh that felt like a stifled scream of relief. They were gone.

I jerked the keys from the ignition and ran the last part of the journey.

An ambulance? Two cop cars and a motorcycle? Whatever was going on, it added up to bad news, and my hunch told me someone was hurt badly. Maybe Luke? It was a sickening thought. After all the good things he'd done for me, the generosity of the guy, for him to get hurt, my one friend, that would be awful. Or what if he was dead? The thought caused me pain, real physical pain deep, deep inside me. I ran and wanted nothing more than to see Luke, wishing we'd never been split up. I remembered all the kind things he'd done, the way he cared for me when I was ill, picked me up at rock bottom, fed me, talked sense to me, sold his Range Rover for me. I wanted to see him so badly, I wanted to see him standing in the middle of the road, smiling and unhurt. 'Luke!' I called to him but only the early morning birds replied.

I reached the place where we'd parked and, to my deepest, darkest alarm, there was no sign of life. Short of breath and panting, I sat on the grass, with my head in my hands. He was dead. That was it. That was him in the ambulance, that's why it wasn't speeding down the lanes, there was no point, Luke was in the back, dead, and I was out here on my own again.

'Daniel?' Luke's voice came from nowhere. I scrambled to my feet; he was in the middle of the road, directly facing me. He seemed like a ghost, like he could vanish as suddenly and quietly as he'd appeared, dissolve into the air and evaporate on the whim of a breeze.

'Luke?'

'Where've you been, Daniel?'

I hurried towards him, holding him in my arms and touching him to make sure he was solid, solid flesh and bone. And not only was he solid, he was damp.

'Has it been raining?' I asked. His shirt was soaking wet.

He delved into my eyes. 'I thought you'd snided off with the money and the car!' Luke didn't sound angry, just as pleased to see me, as I was to see him.

'Luke, I swear on my mother's eyes, I'd never do a thing like that to you. Honestly, I wouldn't do anything to hurt you!'

My hands were red, where I'd been touching him, and so were my arms where I'd been holding him. I looked at the blood that had rubbed off onto me and then at Luke.

'I got jumped by these three lads.'

He was supernaturally calm and there was a tone in his voice I'd never heard before. He was in shock. There was a network of cuts up and down both his arms. I

100

looked him up and down, and tried to hide the horror I felt. 'Let's get you to a hospital!'

He held a hand up to silence me. 'Take me to the car. Let's get away from here, it's crawling with cops, and you don't want to have to explain yourself to them. Do you?'

★　★　★

Blood, once spilled, has a habit of getting everywhere.

I took the wheel and drove around the back roads until we came to the edge of a forest and the sound of running water. There was a deep and fast flowing stream, well off the road and hidden by a broad wall of trees. I felt contaminated as I stripped off by the water's edge and Luke fetched a bag of his own clean clothes from the boot. The blood had seeped through the T-shirt and jeans giving my skin a pink-stained effect and a horror show glow. Luke, who insisted in fetching the clothes, had hardly spoken since getting into the car, saying simply, 'Tell you later!' when I asked, 'What happened? Are you OK? Do you know what that ambulance was there for?' In the end I'd shut up. The last thing he needed was me badgering him. It was my turn to look after him.

I rinsed my T-shirt in the stream, watching with grim fascination, as pink clouds of blood rolled into the path of running water.

I doused my body with freezing cold water, again and again, feeling the chill through the skin to the bone, determined to get the blood stain from my chest. I shuddered and coughed and felt my breath sucked from me as the coldness got a grip of me, but I didn't care, I just had to get clean.

Luke dropped a bundle of clothes and started undressing. The cuts on his arms were more like deep scratches and looked like they'd been there for some hours. There were thin crusts of blood around these red raw welts but, more horribly, there was a very deep stain of crimson from the base of his throat to his kneecaps. His cuts weren't enough to cause such an outpouring of blood. The blood on his skin clearly came from someone else.

I looked at his eyes – faraway blue, summer skies, not quite with it – and dearly, desperately hoped he wasn't going off his head with some severe form of post-traumatic stress.

'Are you OK, Luke?'

'I'm covered in blood.'

I wondered whose it was. He seemed to come back to the present, to the place he was and the person he was with. 'Daniel?' It was as if he'd just seen me.

He walked naked into the middle of the stream and knelt down, dousing himself with armfuls of water and wincing with the cold. I scrubbed at my skin with the backs of my hands and my nails, but the red cast still seemed to be there. I ripped grass from the edge of the stream, rubbed the raw roots and soil into my chest, asking myself over and over, 'Whose blood?' like a silent football chant.

Luke crawled further downstream, to a deeper place where he sat down, facing me, with the water passing over him, like a rock, rooted to the bed of the stream, water bouncing from the curves of his surface.

'Do you want to talk about it, Luke?'

'It was horrible.' He disappeared completely under the surface for a few moments and then sat up, facing me, staring at me, as if he was working out whether he could trust me or not, and then, finally, spoke. 'I came out at about, I don't know, it must've been around two in the morning. It was so hot in there. It was dark and I was just sitting on this grass verge near the tent, minding my own business when this lad came up to me and asked me for a light. I told him I didn't smoke and he turned to walk off. The next thing I know, this rock comes flying out of nowhere and goes this far past my head, lands right behind me. There was three of them. The lad who'd asked for the light and his two mates, running at me really fast; I managed to get to my feet and started running but it was dark and I couldn't see past the end of my nose, I was terrified—' He stopped, leaned forward and dipped his face and head in the water. He lifted his face from the stream and carried on.

'I was running so fast I could feel myself falling forward, out of control, but I could hear them coming up behind me, I could hear them laughing and calling me all the foul names going and I could smell them, sweat, leather, dirt cheap aftershave and cigarettes and I could feel their hands swiping out for me and just getting a touch on my back. And then I just fell. I fell over, there was some bump or hole in the ground sent me head over elbow and two of them fell over, tripping on me. But one of them didn't and he just started laying into me with his feet, but I got up – I don't know how – I got up and started lashing out with my fists and feet and one of them got hold of me from behind and wrestled me down into these, like, brambles or thorns but he must've hit his head on a rock, he just let go and he was out of it, on the ground, unconscious. But the other two were still up, kicking me as I tried to get up again. I think that's how I got all these cuts on my arms, when I was dragged down into the brambles.' He took a mouthful of water and rinsed his gums, spitting out a pink concoction.

'I was up again, Daniel. They were there, one to each side, saying, *Chris, Chris, are you OK, Chris?* That must've been his name – Chris – the one who'd knocked himself out. Know what I said to them, Daniel? I said, *Chris? He's dead, on the ground. Now, who's next?* I could tell, one of them was scared by this but it made the other one even madder.

'I went for the one who was angry. I walked into his kicks and punches, right into him, right up to his face and I sent the head in, full force with the hard part of my forehead. I heard his nose open up and felt . . .' He indicated his body, where he'd worn a damp coat of red. 'All this! The other guy ran away and so I just laid in to the one I'd butted.'

'Was he down?' I asked. 'Was he on the ground?'

'It was a different matter when there were three of

104

them all after me. It was all right for them . . . He begged for mercy. I wanted to kill him. But I came to my senses, Daniel.'

There was a dense silence. I tried to dry myself off with grass and leaves and changed into the clean clothes Luke had fetched from the car, not knowing what to say, feeling dizzy at what he'd told me. 'How are you feeling now?'

'I feel horrible. I feel dirty. And I'm in pain.'

The backs of his legs and arms were covered in bruises and red marks as he stood up and walked around, drying himself in the fresh air. He sat down on the edge of the stream and stared into the sunlight that caught the widening ripples on the water. He held his hands to his face and started sobbing, 'I thought they were going to kill me.'

I sat beside him and placed an arm around his heaving shoulders. 'You were only defending yourself. It was three onto one. The vicious little bastards got more than they bargained for.'

'You don't think I'm a bad person then?' He sounded sad and rather unsure.

'Luke, it was self defence. What were you supposed to do, lie down and let them boot you to death?' I thrust clothes into his arms and stood over him. 'Come on, Luke, get your clothes on! Stand up and get yourself dressed!'

He stepped into his boxer shorts and pulled a white T-shirt over his head.

'They're not your problem, Luke. Forget them!'

'I've got something to tell you,' he said. 'Something bad.' I swallowed and held onto my breath. 'I kicked him really hard in the head, Daniel! And I stamped on his face.' I didn't want to hear but I had to ask. 'Often? How often did you kick and stamp on his head and face? More than once?'

Luke nodded, buttoning the front of his jeans. 'Five or six times.'

'What stopped you?'

'My mother!'

'I'm sorry, Luke.' I was stepping into my trainers, feeling more and more edgy but stifling it. 'I don't really think I follow what you're saying.'

'Remember asking me about my compensation, from the Criminal Injuries Board? My mum, she was murdered by three men, battered to death for the fifteen quid in her purse. They killed her for a fiver each. And I remembered her, suddenly, as I was . . . kicking him, and I didn't want to be as bad as the people who killed her.'

At first it didn't register. I looked at him, seeing him for the first time in a brand new light. 'My mum,' he said, 'and me, we'd only been speaking again for a few months. We'd fallen out, I'd done a runner, but I'd gone home and we'd made it all up. We were getting on better than we'd ever done and then . . .' Luke fell silent and started tying the laces on his trainers. He was crying, silently, long, sad tears streaming down his cheeks.

I saw he was sick and I wanted to make him better, I saw him injured and I wanted to help him heal. He hadn't sounded sorry for himself, he'd sounded like someone who'd been deeply abused but still managed to be kind and decent and sane while the world tormented him. I saw the best person I'd ever met.

'I'm – I'm sorry, Luke.'

'You've got to help me, Daniel. I feel battered by it all. Please, just help me and show me round for a while till I get my bearings.'

'Of course I'll help you, Luke. Whatever happens, we'll stand and take it together. And we'll stay together. We won't split up.'

'Will you drive for now?' he asked, gathering up the dirty and wet clothes. I took a sly look at my black T-shirt and realised it was impossible to tell if the blood was all washed out. I sat at the wheel and waited while he dumped the clothes in the boot. 'You're going to have to help me, Daniel,' he said, sitting beside me.

'Think of me as your brother,' I said. 'Think of me that way.'

'Yes, I will then,' he replied. 'Daniel. I love you, I love you like a brother.'

I started the Escort up and edged onto the empty road. I could feel his eyes rooting to the core of my brain. He was waiting for me to speak.

'Yes, Luke, I know. And I love you the same way.'

13

Sleeping Gas

Luke fell into a death-like sleep, his head tilted forward, his breathing shallow, his whole being static, so I pulled in by a gate to a field full of sheep and turned off the engine. I reached for the door handle and was surprised by the sound of Luke's voice. 'Where'd you get to?' he asked, opening his eyes and touching my arm. 'Where? Where'd you get to?' he repeated the question.

'I drove around for a few hours. I had time to kill while I waited, so I drove around. On my own.'

'Oh!' he said, closing his eyes, falling back to a shallow sleep. I started the engine up. I was restless. I wanted to keep on the move. I had to get going. I had to.

★ ★ ★

It was a good job we were on a lonely road when the Escort let out a deeply worrying series of huge bronchitic coughs, followed by a sharp rally of exhaust fume sneezes. I hoped there was nothing seriously wrong with the car when it began to feel like we were in a go-cart passing over a cobbled street. Luke stirred from his sleep and looked about inquisitively, as the spluttering, wrenching engine stopped agitating and the car simply died.

'You must've been for some ride last night,' he said, tapping the dashboard. 'Look at that. We're out of petrol.'

'Have we got any in the boot, in a can?' I asked, hoping to limit the damage of my blunder.

Luke shook his head and said, 'Nope!'

We sat in silence for some moments, looking out over a wide and pleasant valley. 'That's a nice view,' said Luke, completely unruffled by what had happened.

I cleared my throat and said, 'I'm sorry.'

'It could happen to anyone,' Luke replied, kindly, not looking at me, his eyes and mind absorbed by the broad span of the landscape. 'You know, when you're deep in the countryside, miles from anywhere, the scenery becomes absolutely fantastic.'

'I'll go and see if I can get some juice for the engine then!'

But Luke insisted, 'I'll go. I want a walk to clear my head and wake me up.'

'I'm sorry, Luke.'

He got out of the car and stretched his whole body with feline grace, but looking somehow older, sadder, stranger.

'Luke, I'm sorry about your mum,' I said. 'It must have been terrible for you.'

'It was.'

'I think you've been really brave about it.'

'I think I've had no choice about it, Daniel. I'll see you later.'

I watched Luke march around the corner, eyed the petrol gauge and groaned with embarrassment. I picked up the camcorder and took out the tape I'd made of the rave and inserted the one I'd marked *Weasel, etc.*

I eased my eye over the lens. It hadn't occurred to me to watch what I'd filmed before, and as I sat there with nothing to do, I was filled with mounting curiosity. I pressed the play button and a flock of butterflies rose within me.

There was no sound playback but I recognised the first images straight away; it was the back of Weasel's bus as it lumbered along the motorway, and it seemed both as distant as ancient history and as close as the quickening beat of my heart.

'It's only a video,' I told myself. But it was more than that. The images I saw, that unfolded before me, were my personal memories, pictures normally confined to the shadows of my mind now projected into the daylight of the outside world.

I guessed, as the video rolled, I was about to see things on this tape that would disturb me. My most recent memories were no longer a private matter. Anyone who saw this tape had a lie-proof way into the core of my brain.

A cold hand caressed my skull as the tape rolled on.

At the back window of a beaten-up bus, Kyle was alive and smiling.

14

Video Recall

Kyle smiled at me.

He smiled and waved at me from the other side, through two layers of glass, the small playback window inside the camcorder and the dirty rear windscreen of the bus. I turned the tape off and looked out across the landscape. I reached for my face where he'd lashed out with his small foot and hoped he hadn't suffered, that he'd been unaware of the danger he was in, that he was unconscious before the savagery began.

I turned the tape back and watched him again, smiling at me, waving, a trusting child trying to be friendly. *If people could only see this*, I thought, *they'd get the killer in a matter of hours*.

Slowly, lights started going on inside my head and I sat bolt upright in the seat. Here, in my hands, were the very last pictures of Kyle before his death, before he was murdered. I had a tape that could help the police investigation. Dad always went on about how important TV was for solving crimes like this. If people could only see him! Maybe it'd spark something off in someone's memory. It'd definitely keep Kyle fresh in people's minds and turn the heat up on the scumbag who'd done it.

Fear sloughed off me like a vile, suffocating skin. I felt myself grow as I sat there, spooling the tape back for another look and wished I'd hung onto that newspaper from the Little Chef. As soon as we hit a newsagent's, I decided, the first thing I'd do: Buy all the papers! They'd be sure to have the incident desk phone number.

I pressed *fast forward*, reaching the part where Weasel jumped down from the bus and amazingly, he was even uglier on the tape than he was in the flesh. The video blanked out and came back to the next morning where I'd filmed Weasel emerging from his beauty sleep. Off it went again and then – I hardly remembered filming this – there was a short sequence of Kyle's skinhead mum running after us and having an attack of hysterics. I then remembered it. I'd assumed she was throwing a tantrum because she thought she was missing out on something.

I wound back and watched. It was more than that. I watched closely, she was only a small, ever-diminishing figure on the film but it was clear enough. She was in distress. 'Oh God!' I whispered, realising I'd filmed the moment she'd discovered her child was missing. I watched again and caught the side of Luke's face on video as I turned to face the front with the camera and the sequence of pictures closed with Luke's eyes fixed on the rear view mirror, looking directly at the distraught woman in the fading distance.

There was sudden darkness and white noise bars and then it rolled onto the gathering of the fox hunters and Bowler Hat – Mr Parkinson. I stopped the tape. I'd filmed Luke attacking Parkinson with the baseball bat on the same tape that I'd caught Kyle smiling from the back of the bus and his mum realising he'd gone missing.

I fast forwarded the fox hunting and freeze framed outside The Cat and Fiddle. I pressed *play*. The tape rolled on, releasing its images slowly, the church across the road from the pub, the shadows between the two buildings, the door of the pub which didn't move and then the door bursting open and Parkinson, much the worse for drinking, staggered down the street.

This is a dream . . . a bad, bad dream . . . Parkinson's voice came at me out of nowhere. I looked about, but there was no one for miles and I wondered if hearing this voice was to do with me having a fit. And I remembered the story of a famous epileptic, St Paul, hearing voices as he had a fit on the road to Damascus, on his way to crucify and kick the crap out of people he didn't like.

I pressed *play*. Parkinson mustn't have had a clue we were coming after him. He staggered happily along the street, half on the pavement and half off, as we drew closer and closer. Then, he turned and, as he turned, the edge of the baseball bat came into shot, crashing down on his head. I paused the film on Parkinson's face, scrunched in shock and pain, and his hat hovering like a black cloud as it left his skull. *Play!* We were past him, he was out of shot, there was a wall, a quick shot of The Cat and Fiddle, then I must have dropped the camcorder onto the floor. The tape was running but it was recording the floor of the Range Rover. Luke must've picked the camcorder up at that point; Luke filmed me jumping out and tearing off to fetch the bowler hat rolling around Parkinson's head. I was unblocking his throat but it looked like I was trying to choke him and my scalp tingled as I watched myself turn Parkinson onto his side with my foot. *Sticking the boot in . . .* I crouched to pick up the hat and it looked like I was poking his face with my other hand. I looked up. Luke had zoomed in on my face.

I was looking directly into the eye of the camcorder, somewhere between deep fear and high amusement in my eyes. He pulled back, I was still crouched over the body, bowler hat in hand, a pool of blood seeping from the back of Parkinson's head and then darkness. Luke stopped filming me.

If I hadn't known what had really happened that night, I'd have said it was me who'd attacked him. You couldn't see who'd wielded the bat, but there I was messing with the body, stealing the hat with a look in my eyes like I wasn't quite right in the head. I wondered how would it look to a total stranger, say, for instance, a Detective Chief Inspector leading the investigation into the case?

To the suspicious slice of my brain, son of a copper that I was, it looked like Luke had set me up, that Luke had made it look like I'd attacked Parkinson. *Nonsense*, I told myself. Luke was my best, my only friend in this world. I was so quick to think badly of him. The problem then was me. Luke was a good lad, the best, I told myself, my friend who suffered with quiet dignity and gave everything to me, expecting nothing in return.

I had a nasty mind, a nasty, suspicious mind when it came to Luke, Luke who loved me, Luke the true friend, Luke the brother I never had.

Luke the person I'd known less than a week.

★ ★ ★

It was another two hours before he returned and, when he did come back, not only did he have a full metal can of petrol but a carrier bag of sandwiches and fruit. He was well-pleased with himself, beaming with happiness, as he emptied the petrol into the tank.

'We'll eat and get going, eh!' I don't know why, but, in spite of everything, the look on his face filled me with irritation.

He looked across the valley and started singing his song. Was it the song or the way he was singing it, that made me feel like punching something? My nerves were jangling like wind chimes in a hurricane so I blocked my ears up and wished to Christ he'd shut his mouth.

He looked to the sky where the clouds fell away from the shimmering sun and held out his arm, at a forty-five degree angle, as if saluting the heavens, shielding his eyes from the glare of the light.

'Daniel, it's good to be alive. Don't you agree?' He started singing again, the same lines, and I picked through the words and they sounded a lot like some songs I'd heard on TV.

'Luke!' He wasn't listening, he was humming and staring into the sky. 'Luke!' I was a little louder this time, a little more forceful.

'Yeah?' I'd never seen him look so happy. His lightness of mood wired straight into the heat of my own anxiety, kicking over the coals and raising the temperature higher and higher.

'Where'd you get the tune?'

'I don't know . . . I picked it up on the way.'

'Yeah, well, it sounds a bit iffy, OK!'

He joined me in the front of the car and started eating a sandwich.

'This farmer and his wife,' said Luke. 'They gave me petrol and asked if I wanted something to eat. I said, there's two of us. Human nature can be so wonderful.' He clapped an apple into my hand. 'Now what was that you were saying about iffy?'

'You've no idea where the song comes from?'

'None. It just sounds right to me. When I'm down it picks me up, when I'm up, it's like a love song just for me and the whole of my future.' He ate a little more and asked, 'Why do you think *it sounds a bit iffy*?' He copied me and the effect was uncanny, just as it had been when he took off Parkinson's voice. I hung back and said nothing. 'Daniel?'

'Forget it, Luke. Sing what you want to. It's just me. Sing what you like.'

'Is everything all right?' he asked.

'Fine,' I answered, biting into the apple, without appetite.

'Listen, I've been thinking. Let's go to London. Eh! What do you think?'

'But I thought you were dead against going to London?'

'I was dead against you going to London on your own,

Daniel. But it'd be different, you and me and twelve thousand quid, a different matter altogether. We'll get new clothes and find somewhere to live and . . .' He was tripping over his speech. 'We'll have a ball, we'll have a scream. We'll get a flat together and make money and screw a different girl every day of the week.'

Was he being real? I looked at him closely and saw he seemed sincere enough. I thought on, it must be like a delayed reaction to the shock, following on from his dust up with death. I buried the urge to tell him to shut it and tried to remember all the lousy things that had happened to him to try and whip up a bit of brotherly feeling for him in my heart.

He was trying to offer me some sort of a future at a time when all I really wanted was to sort out the past, so it was hard to feel anything other than plain irritated because he was talking a bit too fast and right through his blowhole.

'What do you say, Daniel?'

I nursed the camcorder in my hands, like a sick and dying pet and replied, politely as polite could be. 'Thanks, Luke! That sounds just great.'

★   ★   ★

Luke was back in the driving seat, windows down, singing along with the rock anthems on the radio, the happiest guy in the world but his mood, his laughter just wasn't contagious. Instead, it drove me deeper down into the gathering black hole that was spreading around me.

I so much wanted to hand the video tape over to the police but there was the Parkinson problem. I had a solution. I didn't know where to start with Luke but I was so pumped up with tension that I just had to face things head on.

'I think there's something you ought to see,' I said.

'What is it?'

I turned the radio off. We were on an A-road, trying to find a turn-off onto the motorway. 'Next chance you get, pull in to the side of the road.'

'Next chance you get, pull in to the side of the road!' It was like hearing my own voice pour out of a different body, a horror film special effect.

'I don't like you doing that. Please don't do that again,' I said.

'Oh, will you lighten up, Daniel!'

I said nothing; his sparky mood was getting harder to tolerate the longer it lasted. It was hard to understand, given that last night he'd nearly been murdered and had only survived by stomping in a bloodbath. But maybe that was it, the key to his jolly mood. Yesterday, he had survived; today, he was alive; tomorrow, which he never tired of singing, belonged to him, tomorrow he would be happy ever after.

I rewound the tape to the beginning and handed him the camcorder.

'I want you to watch this, and I want to talk about it,' I told him. He smiled and bowed his head to view the tape. He didn't make any sound as he watched. He didn't move or react in any way whatsoever, he just sat head bowed over the camcorder absorbing the contents of the tape.

After a long wait, the minutes felt like they'd shuffled themselves into an elastic hour, he looked up and asked, 'So, what do you want to talk about?'

I was astonished. I was astonished and starting to feel very angry. He sat back and smiled. No problem. I took an in-breath and ordered myself to speak slowly and without emotion.

'Did you see who was on the tape?' He nodded but seemed blank and clueless to the place I was drifting towards. 'It was Kyle! I bet they're the last pictures ever taken of him!'

'That's probably so,' he agreed.

'And there's the bit with Kyle's mum, when she must've just found out he was missing.'

'It's terribly sad,' Luke sighed. 'But that's the wonderful thing about video. You capture real life as it's happening, with all its highs and lows. Remember, video tape cannot lie!'

Yes it can, I thought, recalling the section with Parkinson. Yes it can, Mr Frears!

Silence, a long tense silence, and then: 'What are you leading to here, Daniel?'

'I think we should hand the tape over to the cops!'

He laughed very loudly, slapped his legs hard with his open palms, wept with the sheer force of it; his laughter spiralled out of control, a monster feeding on itself and growing stronger with each mouthful of insane noise. He was possessed by insane, naked amusement. 'You're kidding me!' and 'That's a good one!' he squealed, when he could get his breath.

Eventually, and it was a long, testing time, he calmed down and wiped his eyes, rubbed the aching muscles of his face.

'Just for a moment, just a half moment really, Daniel, I thought you were being serious.'

'I am being serious!'

He looked at me, face wide as a child's smile. He looked at me more closely, his face slowly closing down into a frown.

'You want us to walk into a police station and hand over this tape?'

'Yeah.'

'Why?'

'Because it's the last footage of Kyle while he was alive and then there's Kyle's mother on the film. It's useful evidence, it might help jog someone's memory.'

'No.'

'What?'

'No!' He sounded irritated, as if I was a dense and demanding infant child.

'But there could be a single detail on the film that helps catch the killer and closes the case.'

'Don't be stupid.'

'I'm not being stupid. Big cases are usually solved by gathering a load of small details! It mightn't look like anything to you or me.' His body froze in an arch and I felt I could read his mind, screaming, *I'm not listening to this any more!*

The thread of my patience was like an overwound guitar string, one more micro turn of the machine head being enough to send it snapping and whiplashing wherever the force of nature took it. I folded my hands under my arms and clenched my fists, while my back teeth unwittingly ground against each other. Luke looked straight ahead and fell deeper by the moment into the profoundest silence, his mood deteriorating into darkness as he gripped the steering wheel.

'I know what you must be thinking, Luke. There's all that business with Parkinson, but I've thought about that. If you look closely at the tape, you're not implicated. It looks like it was me who whacked him. I'm prepared to take total blame for what happened.'

'But he's dead,' Luke said, coldly, turning on me. 'You're prepared to be arrested and charged and go on the stand for manslaughter then? Just because you happened to catch a kid on film who got killed and you *think* you *might* be able to help the police with their investigation. That's very noble of you.'

'He's dead?' Two small words, two brutal blows, over and over, to the head, to the heart. 'Is he?' I asked. 'Is he dead? Luke, is he dead?'

'I don't know if he is or he isn't, Daniel. But what if you got unlucky and he took a bad turn and pegged out. What'll that make you then? A killer.'

'No, Luke, that makes you a killer. All I'm saying is, I want to help the police get the bastard who killed Kyle and if I've got to face the music over Parkinson I'm prepared to do that! What are you shaking your head for like that?'

'I've got to be honest with you, Daniel, I'm worried about the way you've reacted to this kid's death. You've been . . . different. Strange. It's as if you were personally involved in some way!'

He looked at me, accusingly, and I felt myself turn hot and cold at once. Surely, he wasn't hinting that he suspected me in some way!

'What do you mean?' His words alarmed me and my anger was leaking out. What was he getting at? His words were littered with innuendo and I hated it with a vengeance.

'I mean, you're acting like the kid was related to you. Let me remind you of the facts here. You bumped into him, Daniel, briefly, very briefly. I'm as sorry as you are he died so horribly – don't think you're the only one with any compassion round here – but you're just totally overreacting, mate.'

'Overreacting?' I was shocked, by what he said and the way he said it, as if I was arguing about the referee's decision in a football match. I decided to shut up and let him carry on, find out what else was going on in his head.

'Completely overreacting. There are kids getting killed all over the country, you know, kids getting battered to death at home, kids getting killed off all over the world in fact. You've only got to watch the box to see that. Do you crack up every time you watch the Ten O'Clock News? Do you go into mourning for every starving

African kid you see?' I didn't reply. 'But you're prepared to do time and get raped in prison just because you, *accidentally*, filmed some young kid just before he got his throat slit.' He laughed, bitterly. 'I'm sorry but if stupidity was a crime, Daniel, you should be doing a life sentence with no chance of parole. And you'd deserve nothing less!'

Part of me felt crushed by the enthusiasm of his attack on me and part of me felt embarrassed and unwilling to speak to him ever again. There was nothing inside me other than frozen anger, and as far as he was concerned, it would never thaw. I'd offered to take on board a piece of his wrongdoing, and he'd spoken to me like I was dirt.

He clapped his hands together in a big theatrical gesture, as if he was closing the curtain on the conversation. He smiled at me, his whole body language changing from hostile to friendly, his attitude towards me doing a three-point turn to what it should have been.

'Well, I guess we've just had our first big row,' he laughed.

'I guess so.' I also laughed but my eyes weren't smiling like his were and I spoke silently to myself, *This isn't right . . . this just isn't right!*

'I'm sorry,' he said. 'I just don't want you to do anything . . . to harm yourself.'

'I know, I know.' I know nothing, I thought. I was in shock at the pure venom I'd seen in him, the sheer scorn he'd directed at me. He held his hand out and I shook with him though forgiveness for me was a slow and drawn-out process, and my gesture was a purely hollow one.

It was a game. I was involved in a game now, that meant I had to be smart and shrewd and false. I realised. I had to be like him.

'No hard feelings then?' He now sounded like the person I thought I knew and liked, his whole manner had changed back and he looked at me, waiting for a reply.

'No . . . no hard feelings,' I said, to his smiling eyes.

Luke turned the key and said, 'Fingers crossed!' First time it didn't take but then the engine flared into life and we took to the road.

'I'm only trying to protect you,' he confided.

'I know.' I looked down across the valley and then at Luke, whose eyes were burning into me. 'I know,' I repeated the lie for his benefit and he seemed satisfied with it.

But there was only one thing I knew for sure and it was this single brutal and mindbending truth.

I knew nothing.

15

Over the Sea and Far Away

As the day wore on, it grew steadily warmer, the warmth forming into the kind of heat that set off the faintest scents in everything it touched: rubber, tarmac, metal, plastic, grass, trees, flowers, skin. All day long, the scent on my skin grew closer, the fragrance stronger, the smell of blood sickly and stale. I felt like I'd rolled around in a butcher's window, that there was a rawness around me that no amount of washing could dispel.

'Luke, I want to have a wash.'

'But we had a bath this morning, in that stream.'

'I need a wash badly.'

'We can stop off before we get to London, OK. The roads are fairly clear at the moment, let's take advantage of that.'

There was something else I wanted to do when we finally made our next stop off, something I needed to do rather badly. I was going to ring Dad for a chat. Just to say hello. To see how he was doing. And to ask *what can I do?*

The conversation between us had pretty well dried up with whole stretches of motorway between a brief exchange like:

'Do you want to talk about your mother, Luke?'

'Some other time!'

'OK.'

And then, without warning, he'd laugh, not as maniacally as he had done over the video tape, but with the same unfathomable look in his eyes. And then he'd go quiet and I'd say:

'Something amusing you, Luke?'

'Tell you later!'

'OK.'

I pretended to be asleep, needing time to think, to be as far away from Luke as possible within the space of the old Escort. The matter of handing the video tape to the police may have been closed in his book but in mine it was still wide open and ready to read.

I sighed heavily to give the impression that I was in a deep, deep sleep and decided I'd post the tape to the police as soon as I had half a chance. Luke started mumbling to himself so I kept my eyes closed tight and ears open wide but couldn't catch a word of it.

I didn't want to be with Luke any more. I didn't want to be with him ever again. Not after the way he didn't want to send the tape in, not after the way he spoke to me, not after the way he laughed, not after loads of little things that I'd tried like mad to ignore but had been getting right under my skin and crawling about like a race of mutant super lice.

I turned away from him, in my faked sleep, and wished a few hundred quid could appear in my pocket and then I'd be able to say, 'This is what you've spent on me. Now I don't owe you anything!' But that was a stupid idea, the sort of wishful thinking that makes people queue up for lottery tickets.

I wanted to ring Dad and, maybe, ask him if it was OK for me to come and see him, could he send me a Shuttle ticket, or the plane fare, or something! *I woudn't stay long, just enough to get my head sorted . . .*

Fear was buzzing around the nerveways of my body, like charges of electric current. Fear was stalking the chambers of my heart, inspecting the derelict property and preparing to move in permanently. Fear was lurking in the unseen wings of my mind, waiting for its cue to walk centre stage in my brain and enlighten me on the matter of neverending darkness.

I was seized by the desire to open the door and roll out at speed.

I reached for the door handle and Luke let out a half-scream and a growl that turned me to stone. He sighed and groaned and slowed the car down to a crawl, a crawl that dropped down to the pace of a spaced-out snail. To our left, there was a blue Fiesta, to our right, a white Cavalier. We were all stuck in a bottleneck.

'Daniel!' He spoke too loudly.

I opened my eyes, blinked in the stark sunlight. 'What time is it?' I yawned.

'Five o'clock, five o'clock in the afternoon. Wind your window down!'

As I turned the handle to open the window, I saw the people in the next vehicle looking across, right at us, making a very bad display of pretending they weren't doing just this.

There was a woman in the passenger seat and a man, nearest to me, at the wheel. I made a show of looking beyond them, at the road sign reading *Services ¹/₂ Mile*, so that I could have a closer look at them as I drew my gaze back round.

She looked down at her lap, there was something on her knee. Her husband was also paying a lot of attention to her thighs. What were they looking at?

He was in his mid-thirties, moustache, hair shaved up the back, running to fat and wearing shirt sleeves. He reminded me of the way Dad looked ten years ago and my money said, if I'd had any to gamble, that he was an off-duty copper. PC and Mrs Blue Fiesta.

The windows of the Fiesta went up, the couple talking quickly and, clearly, they were talking about us.

'Have you seen the papers today?' I asked.

'How could I have seen the papers today?' he replied.

'I thought, maybe when you went looking for petrol . . .'

'No. It was the back of beyond out there. There was only the farm. Seen a paper? Don't be a dickbrain.'

She looked directly at Luke, whose attention was lost in the line of traffic ahead. We edged forward. I looked in the rear view mirror, she was raising something for a closer view and I saw the edge of it. She was looking at a newspaper. *They're looking at a photofit!* I thought, feeling the quickening beat of a deep pulse at the base of my skull.

They surged past us and she dropped the paper out of sight, staring dead ahead as they went past. She had a biro in her hand and was writing something on the paper as we came level with them once more. *She's making a note of the number plate!* I could feel my whole body clench like a fist.

I was drumming my hands on my legs and watching them from the very corner of my eye, their heads unmoving, their mouths clattering silently behind the glass, identifying us, condemning us, convicting us. Go ahead, I thought, I haven't done anything . . .

'Do you ever get the feeling you're being watched?' asked Luke, without a hint of any feeling, without fear or anger.

'How do you mean?' I replied.

'I read about this guy, in America, stuck in a car jam like this. He thought the people in the next car were looking across and talking about him, laughing at him.' Luke stopped speaking, gazed directly at the couple next to us, and I waited, having only heard half a story.

'What'd he do?' I enquired, as both lanes moved forward. Luke turned, indicated to the car behind us that he wanted to change lane and with a sharp twist of the wheel, rode diagonally behind the Fiesta, edging much too close, bumper to bumper with it.

'What'd he do?' Luke lapsed into my nasal Liverpudlian dialect and then back into his own unbroken English. 'He got his gun out of the glove compartment and shot them both in the head, several times.'

He made a gun of his hand and fired imaginary shots into the Fiesta, into the backs of their heads. I looked the other way and wished I was on the other side of the

129

planet. I felt the same deep unease I knew as a child when the lights went out and the central heating pipes imitated evil spirits. I decided, there and then, as soon as I was away from him, come what may, it was time to walk!

'Do you know what his name was?' asked Luke. 'This guy who shot his way through the car jam?'

'What was his name?' I wondered if they'd seen him doing his psycho mime, or if the people behind had, or the people to our right.

'His name was Luke Frears! Amazing coincidence that. But there the similarity ends. He was a black man from Michigan and he's now on death row. I share neither of those unhappy conditions.'

'And where are you from?' It occurred to me, he'd never told me anything like this about himself and I, for whatever reason, had never asked.

'All over the place. We moved around a lot. I was born in Glasgow and I suppose, if I had to call anywhere home it'd be Manchester. That's where my mum was murdered. That's where she's buried.'

I could have sworn I caught the merest flicker of a smirk on his face, but I didn't catch it long enough to be certain beyond all doubt. He seemed lost again, in whatever was showing up on the merry-go-round in his head. We were strangers who, in the brief heat of a bogus friendship, had dived far too deeply into each other's lives.

We were edging forward under the bright afternoon

sky but it felt like I was locked under a dark staircase, listening to the front door slamming shut.

The turn-off into the service station was looming up. 'Service station! I want a wash and a cup of tea!' I told him, and the chance to lose him altogether, I thought. The Fiesta forged ahead, making a space between us which Luke closed, quickly and aggressively. 'They've had the same idea,' I said, as PC and Mrs Fiesta indicated left and steered their way out of the jam and up the slip road to the service station.

'Were they watching us, Daniel?'

'Who?'

'Those two in front.'

'No! Definitely not.'

'Just as well,' said Luke. 'For them. I could've sworn they were watching us.'

'You're imagining it,' I laughed, I lied. Why should I tell him anything?

I had some money in my pocket, enough to make a call to France. I squeezed the coins till their edges hurt my fingers.

'Have a look on the shelf, under the dashboard, Daniel!'

I reached out an unwilling hand and poked about in the darkness and there in the space normally reserved for day-to-day junk was a grey metal handgun which I threw back into the darkness as soon as I recognised it.

The Fiesta went one way, losing itself in a series of sudden twists and turns in the spaces between the body of parked cars. Luke reached across and took the gun out. He turned it over, this way and that, as if I was in any doubt as to what it was, and as he slowed to enter an empty parking space, he poked the cold metal barrel into my ribs. I looked down, as he pressed it hard into my bones and imagined the shattering of bone, the eruption of soft flesh, the mess I made at the end of my days.

'I'm sorry, Daniel!' he whispered, in the kind voice he'd used when I first met him. 'But I'm afraid it's all over for you.'

16

Father and Son

I raised my hands, made horse blinkers for my eyes as the metal barrel pressed deeper into my ribs and the cold metal chilled me through.

He clicked his tongue sharply against the roof of his mouth and laughed. My body seized up against the bullet that he never fired. He laughed and withdrew the gun with, 'Realistic or what?'

I opened my eyes and saw the real life humdrumness of the service station, the filling station with its stream of hungry cars, one in and one out, the cashier busy gathering in a constant flow of hard cash.

'Don't worry, it's only a replica. We can hold up the petrol station, if we want. When you've got a gun, you can do exactly what you like. In fact, you don't even have to have a gun, you just have to make people think you have.' He tossed the weapon into my lap and I picked it up with both hands, making sure I didn't touch the trigger. It might have been a replica! It might have been real! I didn't know whether to believe him. I didn't know if he knew, or cared.

'We've no need to rob the petrol station,' I said, calmly. 'We've got loads of money. It's the wrong time of day and the wrong place. There are too many witnesses for my liking.'

'True enough, but when the money runs out, Daniel . . . we do what we have to do to get by. No backing out.'

'Of course,' I lied. Of course not, I thought. I placed the gun back on the darkened shelf and went back in my mind to our first meeting. Everything, I realised, as we sat in that car park, every moment I'd spent with Luke, I would have to go over, check in my mind, double check, question, remember, think and work out.

The scent of blood rose from my skin in a bitter breeze that sharpened my mind and darkened my heart. Had he told me the truth about the three lads jumping him? Had he told me the truth about anything? There was something very wrong with him. Either that, or there was something not right about me.

★ ★ ★

When we queued up at the servery, I noticed Mrs Fiesta was on her own at a table overlooking the car park. 'I wonder where *he* is?'

I spoke my thought out loud, causing Luke to turn and ask, 'Who? You wonder where who is?'

'The person who stole my Nike bag.'

'Why?'

'Nothing, I was just wondering.'

I glanced down and my heart kicked at the sight of his car keys hanging from his back pocket. I smiled at Luke and he smiled back and, as I smiled into his eyes,

I lifted the keys away from him and hid them in my sweating fist.

Mrs Fiesta was looking in our general direction, protected by the distance between us. I wondered, *Where's PC Fiesta?*

'What do you want to eat?' he asked.

'Just a coffee.' My guts felt like they'd been used for knot practice by the boy scouts. They felt so tight that if I swallowed anything solid, combined with the rancid smell rising from my skin, the chances were it'd bounce straight up again. 'Look, I've got to get a wash,' I told him, leaving the queue.

'You've got to eat, Daniel!' I stopped; a middle-aged woman looked fondly at him, my caring older brother.

'I'll see you in a few minutes!' I called, and the outside world screamed past me as I hurried to the central concourse and bought a £4 phone card. I felt like I was sprinting against the natural rotation of the planet and I badly messed up dialling Dad's home number. I slammed the receiver down and watched the green card pop out of the slot. I tried again, deliberately slowing myself down with long intakes of breath.

I had to calm down. I had to slow down and calm down before I talked to Dad. I tapped out 00 33 plus 1 for the Paris area. I squeezed myself as far as I could into the perspex shell for cover, for as I dialled the eight digits of Dad's home number, I felt like the walls and ceiling were beginning to close in on me. I stopped dialling two digits from the end. Was this the beginning of an epileptic fit, sparked by stress? I took a deep draught of air and told myself, No! I dialled the last two and waited for the tone to ring out.

The phone rang out and, on the edge of my vision, I thought I saw PC Fiesta hovering in the middle of the concourse and looking over at me. I turned, as the receiver rasped in my hand, but there was no sign of him. In the quiet moment, between the brash purring, I caught a distant cross wire, a voice pair of animated foreign tongues that sounded like *Cracking up! Cracking up!*

Click. There was no reply, just a silence and, I thought, I've got the answering machine. 'Hello!' I blurted. 'Hello! Hello?' There was no message coming through, but the payphone was eating the units from my phone card, the line was connected.

I saw Fiesta, lurking on the outskirts of my vision, and this time, he was with two uniformed transport policemen. I turned to take a better look and they were heading into the café but there was still no human sound on the receiver as 38 units dropped to 37.

'Hello!' I was nearly crying into the silence. 'Hello!' and was ready to slam the thing down when 'Danny?' weaved into my ear. It was Pascale, her voice breathing down the line like a life-saving whisper, her voice fragile and not her usual confident self.

'Pascale? It's me, Danny!'

'Danny?' There was something definitely wrong. The old expression, *You look like you've seen a ghost* came to mind but turned itself around a little. She sounded like she'd heard a corpse.

'Pascale? Hello, it's me, Danny.'

'Danny!' At last, she sounded like she recognised me. 'But, Danny, you've . . . you're a . . . you're dead!'

The phone turned from hard plastic to thin rubber in my hand, seemed to bend in my grip, as my head swam and heart leaped. The world shrank from around me and I felt encased in naked shock, unable to stand properly, at once sick with shock and giddy with weird rhythms throbbing, *Dead! Dead! Dead!* I leaned against the walls of the booth to stop myself from falling down onto the polished floor which moved beneath me like the deck of a ship on a wind tossed sea.

The units dropped to 28. 'I'm – I am – I'm not dead!'

'Danny? Is that you?' She was crying.

'Yeah, it is me, Danny . . .'

'Danny, what is happening to you?' Good question, Pascale!

'Maybe you can tell me what's happening? Whatcha mean, dead?'

'I'm sorry, I don't understand your English?'

I slowed right down, spoke clearly in a voice clipped of short cuts and devoid of emotion. 'What do you mean, when you say, *Danny, you are dead*?'

'Danny, your father, he has gone back to Liverpool. He has gone back because the news arrived that you had died, that you had run away and killed yourself. You are dead and your father has gone to your mother. You are dead? No? You are not dead! Or is this just another of your father's lies?'

And then she hung up. The line of communication

between us died and I dropped the receiver, taking the card as it popped out.

I laughed, covering my mouth with my hands and staring at the receiver. There was another person hovering, waiting to use the phone but I was entranced, unable to move away from the booth. Dead? What was she going on about? Surely the dead don't panic as I had, don't go hot and cold and laugh quietly when they're feeling like crying loudly.

I drifted away, clicking my thumbs across all four fingers, over and over, as I went, like a mental patient, looking for the reassurance of flesh pressing bone. I was wandering in a shrinking circle in the area between the phone booths and a donut stand, the smell of hot sugar and sizzling, liquid fat knocking me sick.

Dead? What was going on here?

I walked into an overflowing bin, banging my hip sharply, and knocking it over, drawing the puzzled gaze of all around. The bin rolled backwards, losing half its contents, including a grease-stained newspaper. It was the *Daily Mirror* with the headline BUTCHERED, and the picture of him and the words *Kyle . . . slaughtered*.

He was looking at me, his eyes never leaving mine, as I picked up the damp tabloid. I folded his picture up so no one could see and, nursing him in my arms, carried him away.

17

Bitter Truth

In a graffiti-daubed cubicle, I stared at the newspaper, reading the first paragraph over and over, unable to make it over the first full stop.

The mutilated body of traveller toddler Kyle Wolf was unearthed by police in a shallow grave in woodland near Banbury.

Which was as far as I got last time, back in the Little Chef. 'Come on, come on, come on!' I urged myself and dragged my eyes into the next paragraph.

Just under twenty-four hours after his distraught mother, Jade Wolf, 24, sounded the alarm that Kyle had gone missing from their temporary home, a team of local officers found a piece of disturbed ground on the edge of Dunvegan Woods.

The grizzly truth lay just beneath the surface.

Senior Police Officers have ordered a media silence over details of little Kyle's injuries and cause of death though one eyewitness described the body as 'mutilated, atrocities beyond belief'.

I re-read the words in bold print. A media silence?

No one, except the police and the killer, knew what had happened to Kyle, how he'd died.

Yards from the discovery of the body, police recovered an unspecified item of bloodstained clothing believed to belong to the killer.

DCI Judy Parker, the officer leading the investigation, has appealed to anyone who was in the Banbury area around the 14th March, to contact the incident desk on 01865 556677 if they think they have any significant information which may help the police in their enquiries.

'Any information, however trivial, may prove vital in catching the killer,' said DCI Parker.

Like video tapes of the child hours before he died? I should have just taken it to the police without discussing it with flake Frears! *'All calls will be treated in the strictest confidence.'*

The tape was out there in the car. He didn't want me to give it to the police. He was one hundred per cent about that. Yet I did. I did. And I was one hundred per cent about that as well. But I also happened to be in the right.

It was confirmed that three travellers, all arrested in connection with the killing, have been released from police custody without charge.

I didn't need his permission to do what I wanted to do, I didn't need his say so to do what was right.

More Details – p.2, 3,4, 8.

I rolled the newspaper up and placed it in the back pocket of my jeans. No doubt, Luke would be wondering where I was but not only did I have no intention of going back to the café, I had no intention of seeing or speaking with him again.

The world faded away from me as I hurried across the concourse and into the car park. My mind was fixed on a narrow line: Car, video tape, police! Car, video tape, police! I took the hot, wet keys from my pocket as I twisted and turned my way between the rows of cars towards the filling station area.

Behind me, a chorus of voices sounded in the background of a different world, a world apart from the one in which I opened up the driver's door and knelt on the seat, leaning into the back and pulling out the tape marked *Weasel, etc.* from the box.

'Turn on the engine! Turn on the engine!' From the distant voices, a single hysterical scream. 'Turn it on! Turn it on!' It was Luke's voice, followed by a roaring tide of anger commanding him to stop.

I turned around. Luke was pelting towards the car, screeching, 'Turn on! Turn on! Turn on!' He was being closed down by a scrum of transport coppers with PC Fiesta bringing up the rear of the pack.

His eyes, wide, animal, frightened beyond reason, met mine and he howled, and cried like a thousand tormented demons screaming to the edge of a cliff. He tried to gaze his way into my mind, pierce my eyes with his and carve his will onto the part of my brain that told me what to do. I stared back, not flinching from the rising rage in his face and said, 'No!'

His face twisted into a vile mask, so out of shape with the face I recognised as his that he could have been a different person altogether, except for the eyes which held onto mine in a battle of wills.

'He had his throat cut,' I said to myself, remembering Luke's description of Kyle's injuries, back in the toilet at the Little Chef. ' . . . And he was stabbed in a frenzy, with a long blade, with a serrated edge.' Luke knew how he'd died, yet there was a news blackout on the details. Luke knew he hadn't been interfered with, sexually. Even though there was a news blackout and the only people who knew these things were the police and the killer.

As the awful truth sank in, his face twisted back to something more familiar, but it was too late. In my mind's eye, I'd marked him down, for future memory, with the contorted, the monstrous and terrifying look I'd just seen.

In a speck of an instant, the transport policeman nearest Luke caught his legs sending him flying onto the bonnet of the car, his mouth wide, the same wail still thundering from inside him. His eyes ran into mine, and I could tell he wanted to kill me.

There was another copper on top of Luke, pressing him down on the bonnet and throwing his arm up his back with unrestrained force. In the next speck of the same instant, the world around me was blotted out by bodies surrounding the Escort and the driver's door nearly came off its hinges, while another pair of hands dragged me out and lifted me onto the boot of the car like I was some kind of rag doll. My spine cracked as I made impact with the metal and ripples of hot and cold pain coursed through me over and over.

The video tape and the car keys were still in my hand but the pain and the voices barking at me made me lose control of my arms, and I dropped both to the ground. I concentrated all my being into stifling my pain and I my eyes shot open as I was lifted off the boot and thrown face forward and spreadeagled against the car next to the Escort. My hands were cuffed behind my back and I was made to stand upright.

'I'm arresting you for the attempted murder of George Parkinson. You don't have to say anything but anything you do not say now but mention later on, the court may decide failure to mention now may be used against you!'

A crowd was gathering on the station forecourt, another outside the concourse.

Luke stared wildly at me as three of them marched him away, and hissed, 'Murderer!'

The boot of the Escort clicked and slowly, of its own accord, swung wide open.

'What's your name?'

'Danny Anderson!'

As they dragged me past the open boot of the car, I looked on in amazement. In the corner, between a toolbox and a bundle of newspapers, was my Nike bag.

18

Arrested

For every case of a stolen bike that turns up safe and sound in a police station, it's a fairly safe bet that there'll be about five lives about to go inside out and down the pan.

The Custody Sergeant, Stein, repeated my name, 'Daniel Anderson! Daniel! Danny!'

'You're entitled to have a social worker with you during the interview . . .'

'I don't want a social worker.'

'Until your parents get here, Danny, you're entitled to have a social worker with you . . . In the eyes of the law, you're still a child. As you're under the age of seventeen . . .'

'I want a solicitor!'

'Of course,' he said. He showed me a list of names and told me, 'The duty solicitors, take your pick!'

He was a tall, thin man with long thick-knuckled fingers, hands like spades which offered me the list of lawyers. A burning sensation came and went, up and down the pathways either side of my spine. I jabbed a finger, anywhere, on the list and announced, 'That one'll do!'

'Listen,' he said, quietly. 'While you're here, Danny, I'm in charge of you, I'm responsible for you, your welfare's my business. If you have any problems . . . are you listening to me, sunshine?'

'I am, yes, I'm listening, Sergeant.'

'You let *me* know. How are you feeling?'

'All right,' I replied. 'Terrible,' I added.

'You walked in like you were in pain . . .'

' . . . I'm fine, really I am, I just want to tell the detectives everything I know, honestly I do . . .'

'Don't worry, you'll get your chance. I'm going to take you down to the cells for a while, until the detectives are ready to question you. But before we go, let's have the laces from your trainers . . .'

'I'm not going to kill myself, Sergeant.'

'You're not going to get the chance to. Laces . . .'

I winced but stifled it on the way down. My back took a hammering when they dropped me on the car.

'I'm innocent,' I said, looking up to the Sergeant.

'Then you've nothing to worry about, have you, Danny?' I looked at him and saw that he didn't really believe me or himself. 'C'mon, let's have those laces.' He threw them onto the desk with the rest of the gunge from my pockets.

'Did you say my parents are on their way?'

'Yes.'

'Both of them?' I asked. He nodded.

'Come on, let's get going.' I followed him to the cells.

★ ★ ★

You are born, you suffer, then you die . . . I am a raper . . .

145

Man U. Champions '93-'94. The wit and wisdom scratched into the flaking paintwork on the cell walls by those who'd been in this part of the police station before me.

My Nike bag in his car boot! The mere thought of it provoked a pain in my guts that was almost as strong as the one growing across the breadth and span of my back. I cried for half a second and said, 'No, no, no!' quietly to myself, my hands wrestling with each other, until I banished the image of the bag and the pain in my head and heart ebbed away and a billowing numbness settled around me. Numb, I liked it, it was a good place to be.

I sat on the hard bench, settled my shoulder against the wall, and stared at the peephole in the cell door, wondering which was the worse noise, the lunatic in the cell next to mine swearing at full volume in a never-ending stream of hatred or the quiet voice inside my head asking quietly, 'Are you blind and deaf as well as just plain stupid?' Violent, smiling lunatic Luke? I wondered where he was now and what fictions he was weaving.

I wanted to cry but couldn't. Then, I wanted to scream but didn't. And, I wanted to go home but . . . it just didn't bear thinking about.

Next door, the ceaseless swearing suddenly stopped and I took the chance to try and rest. I threw my legs on the bench and lay down, closing my eyes tightly and pressing my aching head against the coolness of the seat. The peephole in the heavy metal door opened and keys rattled in the lock. A uniformed constable came in with a Styrofoam cup of milk and a cheese roll wrapped tightly in clingfilm.

'I don't want anything to eat!' I told him. 'I'm not hungry.'

'We've got to feed you,' he replied. He placed the food on the floor and the milk beside it. 'We're obliged to give you food,' he commented on his way out.

But fear had turned my mouth into a dry cave, so I made my way to the cup of milk and drank it down in three gulps.

Next door, the litany of abuse kicked off with renewed vigour and, once more, I asked myself, this time out loud, 'Are you blind and deaf as well as just plain stupid?'

★ ★ ★

At around ten o'clock – I could tell, I could hear the music from the BBC news playing in a room somewhere in the police station – Sergeant Stein led me to Interview Room 2 and introduced me to the duty solicitor, Mrs Watson, a woman with an air of urgency and a look of Charlie Chaplin in a thick red wig.

As she threw back the pages on a spiral bound notepad, she glanced up at me every now and then, and it was clear she was thinking, *Innocent or guilty?* She stopped fussing with her paperwork, pulled out a packet of Rothmans and, leaning across the table, offered me a cigarette. 'Danny?' She jigged the cigarettes under my chin a little.

I shook my head. 'I don't smoke.'

'Do you want the good news?' she asked. I looked at her. Did I want to hear some good news?

'Yeah, tell me the good news, Mrs Watson.'

'Your mum and dad are on their way down here from Liverpool. This must be very traumatic for you, Danny. Is this your first time in a police station?'

'As a suspect for a crime, yeah. I've been to Admiral Street and Garston stations loads of times to see Dad. Dad used to be in the police, the Merseyside police.'

'Oh well,' she said. 'Most parents in their situation haven't seen the inside of a police station before, so it won't be *that* strange to them.'

'I'm sure it'll be a massive consolation to them, Mrs Watson.'

She iced over and started playing with her notepad, speaking, as if thinking out loud. 'Son of a former police officer? The tabloids will love that.' She arched her eyebrows and whistled a low thin note.

'When am I going to get out of here?'

She pitched back with a gloomy, 'Well, they can hold you for forty-eight hours – that's two whole days . . . They can hold you for forty-eight hours and then they have to charge you. If they charge you, they take you to the magistrate who then gives you a set time – say, seven days, in police custody or releases you on bail. Though, if they do charge you, I don't think you've got a hope of bail. So, short answer to your question, at best two days, at worst, well, whatever . . .'

She turned to her notepad, clicked her pen into action and asked, 'What have you said to the police so far?'

'Nothing much. Where it counts, I've exercised my right to remain silent.'

'Good thinking, Danny. Smart move. Next question, don't lie to me now. Did you do it?'

'I haven't done anything. I'm completely innocent.'

She lit the cigarette she'd been toying with, in her left hand, for a minute or so and blew a stream of smoke into the air which hung over me like an icy blue cloud.

'They're going to take you in for questioning soon. You answer yes for yes, no for no and if you aren't sure, you say, *I don't know!* Don't supply any unnecessary details and don't go off the point. Keep to the question, yes, no, I don't know. If you need time to think, stop and think, if you don't understand a question, tell them, *I don't understand the question!*'

'What's going on, Mrs Watson?'

'You understand, you've been arrested and taken in for questioning with a serious crime?'

'For attacking George Parkinson! How can they say it was attempted murder?'

'They can call it what they like. Where do you draw the line between GBH and attempted murder? Between murder and manslaughter? It's not so clear cut, Daniel. I'm sure they'll get realistic and drop it down to GBH. Anyway, the Parkinson business, it's just glue to keep your feet in custody while they sort themselves out!'

She'd already exhausted the good news and I could see bad news written all over her face, bad news waiting to come straight at me, from her mouth, like the scalding steam from a runaway locomotive.

'They think, they believe . . . they're connecting it with the Kyle Wolf killing! You're a prime suspect. Or, you and your friend are, I should say.'

Flesh turned to stone, blood to ice. I looked at her and shook my head very slightly. 'No, not me.'

'Don't worry, if you're innocent you've got nothing to fear. They've got a lot of forensic evidence. They've even got a bloodstained jacket.' Mrs Watson wasn't looking either very happy or at me. 'How long have you known your friend, Richard Pike?' she asked.

'Richard Pike? His name's Luke Frears.' Another of his deceptions fell coldly from my lips and Mrs Watson shook her head. 'It's Richard Pike!' she said.

'He's not my friend at all. I hardly know him. Yes I was with him, for a short time. About a week.'

I pressed my forehead against the edge of the table and stared at a hardened piece of chewing gum on the floor.

A moment of utter clarity came and went through my head and a picture formed of Luke standing tall and smiling wildly, soaked in blood with the tale of being attacked by three lads, tripping from his lying tongue, and the blood that had soaked off from him onto my skin and my clothes suddenly felt wet and fresh and sticky. I accidentally bit my tongue as it dawned on me that the blood I'd washed from myself meant there was more to come, the smell that had plagued me all day long came back in an overwhelming blast and caught the back of my throat.

'And who was that victim?' I wondered out loud.

'Pardon?' she asked. She was looking at me now, I

could feel her eyes burrowing into the crown of my skull. 'I'll guide you through the initial interviews and do the best I can for you, but you're going to need a good barrister. A very good barrister.'

There was a knock on the door, and Stein appeared in the doorway. He looked at Mrs Watson, they were clearly very familiar with each other.

'You're going back to the cell for a short while and then you're back here,' she informed me, as she packed her bag away. I looked at the chewing gum, black and stone-like on the floor, unable to suffer pain or feel the explosions of pain and anxiety that were going off inside me every other moment, and envied it.

'Anything else? Are they linking any other crimes?' I mumbled.

'No? Any you want to tell me about?'

I thought I'd fainted for the merest moment. I was paralysed in the middle of a dark wilderness with fireballs raining down on my naked head. I was in the multi-screen cinema, back home, watching myself, up on the big screen, Little Me crying for Big Me, real life turning into a moment in a movie, then back to ice-cold reality.

I wanted to run away so badly that it hurt like a crack on the head and a kick in the face, when I realised there was one thing I could never run away from. Myself.

'Anything else I ought to know about?' she asked, her voice clipped, and I shook my head and mouthed the word '*No!*'

'No?' she said. 'Then, I think that's about it. That's enough. For now.'

19

Interview Room 2

I was expecting to be questioned by a pair of lard belly detectives from the C.I.D. murder squad, a pair of baggy-eyed baldies, smelling of fags and bacon sandwiches, looking for a quick confession and a quick cab ride to the nearest pub to celebrate an open and closed case.

Instead, I was led to the Interview Room by Stein to meet a woman called Parker and a man called Waites, a couple who could pass themselves off as a male and female daytime TV presentation team.

My parents were sitting side by side on a pair of stiff plastic chairs and, as they turned their heads together to look at me, it suddenly felt like a lifetime since I'd seen them. They both looked many years older than the picture I held of them in my head, even though it had been just over a week since I'd seen Mum and under a year since I'd last clapped eyes on Dad.

'Hello, Mum . . . Dad . . .' It dawned on me that it had been over two years since I'd seen them together and a lot of murky water had flowed under the bridge since that unhappy night.

They forced a pair of matching, yet clearly faked smiles but they looked blitzed with shock, like they were caught in an overwrought nightmare, waiting for the alarm clock to wake them up and make it all go away.

'Sit down, Daniel!' Waites indicated a chair, and I did as I was told.

I could smell cigarette smoke and expensive perfume hanging on Mrs Watson and the cocktail of aromas made me feel like being sick. I clenched my teeth and covered my mouth with my hands.

'You understand why you're here, Danny?' Waites lobbed the question at me from the back of the room, like an opening serve from base line in a grudge game of tennis.

'Yes, I understand why I'm here. I'm going to be formally charged with attempted murder?'

'Tell us about the night in question. Tuesday, 14th March.' Waites sat down across the table from me, as Parker leaned closer to me. *Go on*, her body seemed to murmur, *tell us all your secrets . . .*

'Why ask me? Why don't you ask . . .' I nearly said *Luke*. 'Why don't you ask Richard Pike?' I said. 'He's the one who attacked Parkinson.'

'Because we're asking you, Danny,' said Waites, with a dreadful smile. 'That's why!'

'Tell us, tell us what happened!' Parker's face was nearly touching mine. I leaned back, as far away from her as I could go, and looked at the space behind her head.

'Richard was angry with George Parkinson so he drove past him and smacked him on the head with a baseball bat. I didn't know he was going to do it, I didn't think it was a good thing to do and I wish it had never happened.'

'Why was Richard angry with George?'

'Because George laughed at Richard earlier in the day.'

'Because he laughed at him?' Waites looked perplexed.

'Did you hit George with the baseball bat?' Parker tilted her head at an odd angle and looked at me at a spot between my eyes.

'No, I did not hit George with the baseball bat,' I replied, looking to the same spot between her eyes.

'That's not what we've been told . . .' Waites informed me.

'Richard Pike says you were the one who hit George . . .'

'So, whose idea was it to attack George Parkinson?' asked Waites, his fingers locking to form the roof of a church.

'He told me his name was Luke,' I sighed heavily. 'It was Richard's idea,' I went on. 'I didn't know he was going to hit him with the bat.'

'Because he laughed?' Parker's voice was loaded with disbelief.

'Yes, strange as it seems, because he laughed at him.'

'Was that the usual sort of thing that angered the co-accused? Laughter?'

Waites sounded like a kind uncle, trying to sort out the rights and wrongs in a kindergarten fist fight.

'I couldn't begin to explain that person's actions,' I said. 'I don't know him. He picked me up a week ago in a service station and we've been hanging around together since then. I realise, too late, he's a mental case, a psycho!'

'That's a very serious allegation, Daniel!' said Parker.

Waites asked, 'Psycho?'

What was the point? It was only a matter of time before they saw the video tape.

'You'll see. There's plenty of evidence in the car. I wanted to send you the tape. That was what I was doing when I was arrested. Making a run for it with the tape. I was prepared to say it was me who hit Parkinson to get that tape to you. How about that?'

'What tape?' asked Parker.

'You're not really interested in the Parkinson business, are you?'

'What do you mean, Daniel?' Waites oozed concern, calm, cop logic.

'You want to know about Kyle Wolf. You think that the two cases are linked. They are. It's a long story but . . . I only realised, just before I was arrested, he – Richard Pike – he told me things about the way the kid died that only the police and the killer could've known.'

There was a quiet in the room, the sort of quiet in which you imagine you can hear the fabric of the walls rubbing against itself and the corners pressing themselves together. 'Then there's the video tape . . .' I said, softly.

'Tell us about the tape, Daniel?' Parker burrowed.

'How's Kyle's mum?'

'You mentioned a tape? A video tape?'

'I filmed Parkinson being attacked. Not that I knew it was going to happen. I had no idea. I was just pointing the video camera. But on the tape, there's something else . . .'

155

My mind turned upside down and all the logic and ordered memory fell into a whirlpool of confusion.

'I understand what's going on here,' I said. 'You've already watched the tapes. You're being vague because you want to give me the rope you hope I'll hang myself with.'

'Tell us about this *something else*?' Waites asked.

'What else?' I couldn't make out which one asked. I was consumed by the image of Kyle looking from the back of the bus, waving to me.

'Kyle . . . I filmed him the day before he died.' His image dissolved. 'We – Richard Pike and me, we argued. I wanted to hand the tape over, I was in the process of doing that when I was arrested . . .'

There was a sharp knock at the door and a plain clothes detective entered with an urgency that drew Parker across the room for a bout of hurried whispering. From the quickness of their voices and their attitudes, I could tell something significant had happened.

I turned and looked at Mum and Dad. Mum looked at me, hurting beneath her smile but Dad's eyes were fixed on the drama in the doorway.

'Mum . . .' I said, not quite knowing what I was going to follow this with.

Parker drew her hand across the air in a cutting motion and Waites leaned towards the cassette's microphone.

'At a quarter past twelve, DCI Parker and DC Waites terminated the interview with Daniel Anderson.'

'Daniel!' It was Parker. 'You're going back to your cell

now. We'll pick up the questioning, later on, maybe; probably, tomorrow morning.'

'You've got the video then,' I said to Parker.

She nodded. 'Some video evidence has come to light.'

I'd rumbled their opening game plan. If only I'd been as smart around whatever the bastard's name was.

Mum watched me go with a helplessness that made me forget my own feelings about the situation for a moment. I tried to smile as I looked about. Where was Dad for her? Somehow or other, he'd made his way out of the room and was absolutely nowhere to be seen.

When Stein stuck the key in the cell door lock, I felt a deep urge to throw myself to the furthest corner of the room and beg, 'Don't lock me up!' I somehow managed to hang on to my dignity and turned the plea into a question, 'My mum, is she OK?'

'Well, y'know, it's hard to tell . . .' He pointed inside the cell. 'Bedtime!'

I walked inside, feeling the weight of his eyes on me. I turned. He was staring at me, perplexed.

'What?' I whispered. 'What is it?'

'Did you kill that kid then?'

'No!'

'Do your best to sleep, you'll need your wits about you tomorrow.'

I opened my mouth to speak, to ask him if he'd stay and listen to the whole story.

But it was too late. The door of the cell closed in my face, and on the other side, the key turned with an echo like I'd never heard before in my life.

20

Morning Chorus

I can't recall falling asleep, only a sense of disbelief that I'd actually managed to do so when I was woken up by the morning chorus of the shouting in the cell next door.

I'd slept sitting up on the bench with my shoulder and head pressed to the wall and the whole of my back felt like it had been walked across by an army of sumo wrestlers. My body tensed instinctively at the memory of being slammed against the boot of the car when I'd been arrested.

I unbuttoned my shirt and, carefully, slid my arms out of it. There was a bluey black contour across the span of my shoulders, heavy bruising that reached the backs of my arms. As I slept, the pain had blossomed and taken over.

As I saw the peephole rise and fall and heard the keys rattle in the lock, I sat back down on the bench. The cell door swung open. It was Sergeant Stein and with him was a man in a dark suit, carrying a black bag.

Stein spoke. 'I noticed he couldn't walk well, I thought it best to get him checked out, Doctor!'

'Turn around,' said the doctor, eyeing the bruised horizons across my shoulders. He said nothing but stared grimly at the picture of internal bleeding across my spine and upper back.

'How did this happen?' asked the doctor.

'Yesterday afternoon, when I was arrested...' I replied. He touched my back lightly but the pain was sudden and shocking.

'How are you feeling, Danny?' Stein moved so that he could look into my eyes.

'X-ray job!' said the doctor.

'Sore!'

'Why didn't you say something yesterday?' asked Stein.

'Look, they threw me on the boot of the car. I don't want to make a fuss, I don't want to make a complaint, I want to co-operate...'

'He'll have to go to hospital,' the doctor said.

I shook my head and said straight to Stein, 'I'll say it was an accident!'

As Stein helped me into my shirt, Waites and Parker walked into the doorway of the cell.

'Daniel Anderson,' said Parker. 'On Tuesday 14th March, at Cotterford in the County of Oxford, I am charging you with the unlawful act of Grievous Bodily Harm against George Parkinson...'

As she carried on talking, her voice became a blur. I wasn't listening properly.

Stein leaned into me. 'Do you understand the charges, Danny?'

'I understand . . . that this is all wrong . . . I understand that.'

★ ★ ★

'Does that hurt?' Dr O'Hara, an elderly-looking woman, in a pure white coat and horn-rimmed spectacles, and a saintly face – a saint who if pushed was ready and able to enter an arm wrestling competition with Lucifer – pressed her fingers on either side of my spine, sending spasms of pain up and down my back.

I answered with a yelp and she replied with, 'How did this happen?'

'I fell over . . .'

'Really?' She clearly didn't believe me. 'Were you resisting arrest?'

'No.'

'Raise your arms out in front of yourself!' I raised them a little way with some effort and a deal of pain.

There was an armed policeman in the corner of the room, his face was bathed in shadows that fell from the peak of his blue baseball-style cap.

'Doctor? While I'm here, could you do something for me?'

'What is it?'

'I think I might have had an epileptic fit.'

'In the cells?'

'No, before I was arrested. I think so, but I can't trust the person who told me. Could you do a test or something to check?'

'Yes, we can do that for you. We can't test and prove or disprove but we can show what's likely to have been. Eyewitness account is the thing. You don't trust the person who saw you?'

'No, I don't'.

'The co-accused?' I nodded my head very slightly.

She turned to the guard. 'We're going to X-ray!' Burning pains, stabbing pains and shooting pains carried on a merry dance up and down the channels of my back and, suddenly, the simple task of walking was no easy thing.

'Daniel, do you talk in your sleep?'

'I'm told so.'

'Then someone . . . the co-accused may have seized on a deep-set fear of yours. Perhaps.' She pointed at my spine. 'I don't think there's anything chipped or broken. I think your ligaments have been damaged. Badly. It's reparable with rest. You'll have to stay in bed for a while.'

★ ★ ★

I sat facing a green VDU with two electrodes taped to my skull, watching the electrical activity in my brain being recorded as a jagged line of sharp peaks and lows, like a young child's rapidly drawn version of a range of narrow mountains.

'What's happening?' I asked Dr O'Hara.

'Your brain's full of nerve cells, like little switches that send out pulses of electricity. The wires taped to your head send the pulses into the machine. The machine records them and sends them out on . . .'

She pulled a strip of paper from the machine, a print out of what was happening on screen. 'This! It's called an encephalogram.'

She studied the paper and showed it to me as she did

so. It looked like a jagged scrawl by someone trying to get the ink flowing in a biro.

'Epileptic?' she said. 'I don't think so, Daniel.'

I took the print out and stared at the line which meant zip all to me.

'He's been having you on,' she told me.

'Yeah?'

'Oh yes, I'm sure he has.'

21

Sleepless

I was placed in a clean comfortable side ward, a whole room to myself in what must have been an overcrowded and noisy hospital, with an armed guard outside the door, to stop people from getting in, and an armed guard in the corner to stop me from getting out.

The X-ray showed no bones were broken but my ligaments were badly torn and I was on heavy doses of painkillers to ease the stabbing and burning, the biting and grinding that was going on up and down my spine, shoulders and lower back.

I lay back on the pillows and looked back up at the white tiles on the ceiling, wondering where Luke was, what lies he was telling about me and just how many lies he'd told me in the brief time we'd been together.

I pictured my Nike bag, stuffed into the boot of his car and retraced my steps from the Liverpool to London bus as it heaved into the service station and right the way into the toilets, the row of hunched backs standing at the urinal, stupidly dropping my bag outside the cubicle as I went inside . . . he must have been one of the men at the urinal!

I pictured his feet slithering across the polished floor with the speed and agility of a primeval snake, his hand snatching away what was mine, his grin, his eyes.

Parker and Waites were standing at the foot of my bed. How long they'd been there, I had no idea. I was lost in the eerie wisdom that I'd been picked by an evil hand for a future I had no control over.

'Yes?' I said, as if they'd dropped in to see if I wanted a newspaper. A woman with a familiar face appeared behind them and made her way to me, extending a hand. Mum was there, right behind her.

'Miss Kerr,' she said. This rang a bell. I sat up and shook her hand.

'Miss Kerr of Hough, Machin and Kerr?' I asked. 'You handled Mum's side of the divorce, right?'

'That's right, Danny, but I'm highly experienced in criminal law and I have access to the finest barristers in the country.'

'That's right, Danny,' Mum added, nodding.

'Believe me,' Miss Kerr carried on. 'I'm just here to hold your hand and guide you through. Your mum and I, we're more like friends than solicitor and client, and she insisted, she wanted me to represent you.'

'We trust her,' Mum insisted, as she stood shoulder to shoulder with Miss Kerr. But I didn't say anything for a while. 'Danny?' Mum urged me to speak.

'Miss Kerr, there's a bit of a difference between splitting up the wedding presents and a case of murder.' I locked into Parker and Waites. 'I know,' I said to them. 'I know *you* haven't mentioned murder yet. But that's what you're here to talk about now, isn't it? Murder?'

'We've seen the video,' Waites said.

'The video I was trying to get to you when I was arrested,' I replied.

'We know you were responsible for the attack on George Parkinson.' Parker had difficulty in concealing the smug edge from her voice.

'Do you mean me? Or do you mean me and Luke, or *Richard* I should say? Because if you do, you're wrong on both scores.'

'We've got the tape, Danny.'

'You've not watched it properly, have you? Not yet? I was holding the camera when Luke smacked him. I stopped him choking on his tongue and . . .'

This was, now, small talk of course. Parker clicked open the locks on her case and produced a brown card file.

'Tell us about Kyle Wolf, Danny?' said Parker. 'You knew him, didn't you?'

'Briefly. I met him the day before he died, before he was murdered. I shot some video footage of him. It's on the same tape as the Parkinson thing.'

'What happened when you met him?' Waites was in confidential, best buddy, voice. 'Tell us, Danny.'

'I met him, I liked him, he was a nice little lad. I felt sorry for him living with the travellers. I didn't really get to know him.'

'Did he do anything to annoy you?' Waites asked. I shook my head which was growing heavy with all sorts of fear and sorrow.

'Can you answer the question verbally,' prompted Parker.

'No, he was a nice little kid. We waved to each other through the windows.'

Parker showed me a photograph. It was of me, bent over Kyle as he lay on the ground. I remembered it well. I was helping him up but it looked like I was about to strangle him.

The flash of Luke's camera went off inside my head throwing a brilliant white cloak of illumination into a darkened spiral of my mind and I was thrown back into the traveller camp when I took Kyle's hands in mine and his foot lashed out and caught me on the chin. A light flashed from a short distance away, then Kyle wandered away.

''Bye 'bye, Mister Mister.'

''Bye 'bye, Kyle Kyle!'

'Are you OK?' Luke's voice seemed to break out of my skull and fill the room with mocking echoes. 'Are you OK?'

In the gathering night of the travellers' camp, the flashlight of his camera flared as he took another photograph, his face unnaturally white, his smile fixed.

I remembered. I remembered these things as if they were happening to me there and then.

He'd photographed me with Kyle in the same way as he'd taken video tape of me over Parkinson's body, in an attempt to make me look like the monster of the moment. And the horrible thing was, the evidence looked completely damning.

I was reaching for Kyle's hands, I recalled, to help him

up, but looking at the picture I could have been going for his throat, or his eyes, or any other part of him.

I looked around the room, at Miss Kerr, at Waites, at Parker, at the ceiling, at the floor, anywhere but the picture, yet my eyes were drawn back there and on second impressions, the image looked even worse.

'I was helping him. I was helping him up. I was trying to help him up from the ground by taking his hands in mine.'

'No you weren't, Daniel.' Parker sounded irritated now.

'Yes, I was,' I reacted.

'We know what you were doing, Daniel, on that occasion, in that picture.' Waites was almost whispering under his breath. 'You were trying to abduct Kyle.'

'No!'

'But it didn't work out that time, did it? Your friend, Richard Pike, disturbed you, took that picture of you, didn't he? He saved Kyle that time, didn't he?'

Parker's eyes were waiting for me as mine returned from the false evidence in that small rectangle she held under my nose.

'I didn't touch Kyle, not to hurt him.'

'You're sounding like an old record, Danny, stuck in the groove, repeating the same old thing, again and again and again!' Waites stifled a yawn and sighed, 'That picture was taken just hours before he was killed.'

'What were you doing to him, Daniel?' asked Parker.

'Helping him up!'

'What were you planning on at that point? What was going through your mind?'

'I was thinking, get the kid up, if the grass is wet he'll catch a cold!'

Their voices drifted in and out of each other, reaching across the table like a succession of open hands, slapping me square in the face.

'Had you actually decided to kill him at this point?'

'Is that what you were going to do, in that picture? Kill him?'

'No!'

'Were you going to take him away and kill him because he kicked you?'

Parker raised her hand enough to cause a silence to descend on the room, to stop the flow of interrogation. After a few moments, she said, 'I'm getting a little tired of all this . . . lying! Shall we show him the other picture?'

'You may have read in the papers, we found an undisclosed item of clothing, soaked in the victim's blood, near the body.'

Parker slid the next picture from her file, looking studiously at the image as she did so, showing me only the white side, tantalising me and then slowly turning the picture over so that I could see. It was my brown suede jacket, splattered with blood, dripping and swimming in dark, dense pools of blood.

'Recognise it, Daniel? It was found two metres away from where Kyle was murdered,' said Parker. 'Is that your jacket?'

'It was burned. Richard burned both of the jackets.'

'Is that your jacket? Answer the question.'

'It looks like it. It's similar. It can't be.' I looked closely and groaned.

'It is your jacket?' Waites repeated the question. It was my brown suede.

'That's . . . my jacket.' It was hitting me hard, my life, my hopes for the future, my dreams of doing anything nice or useful or normal, it was all over.

She was sliding another picture from the file.

'Another one?' My voice was loaded with utter disbelief.

'This is a picture of the knife used to murder Kyle Wolf. It was uncovered ten metres from the body. The fingerprints on it correspond with the fingerprints you gave at the Station last night.'

'Do you recognise the knife, Danny?' asked Waites.

'Yes, it's a carving knife from my mother's kitchen. I packed it in my bag when I left home. The bag it was in was stolen . . . by . . .'

'Daniel Anderson!' Parker's voice invaded me. 'I'm charging you with the murder of Kyle Wolf!'

22

Parents

I didn't hear them coming in and, when I realised they were in the room, they were at the foot of the bed, staring at me. 'Danny?' Mum broke the silence.

'It's nice to see you,' I said. 'Thanks for coming to see me.'

'Danny!' Dad said, his voice, this one word, telling exactly what was going on inside his head. It was the same voice, only darker and deeper, that I'd heard when he was called to collect me when I was caught with a stolen copy of Madonna's *Sex* on the pavement outside HMV. *Is it really you in this much trouble?* Yet again, the son of a copper had turned him into father of the criminal and I found I just couldn't look at the man.

Mum sat down beside me on the edge of the bed and held my face in her hands. 'How's your back?' She smiled at me, she was putting a very brave face on. 'Danny,' she spoke softly. She smiled at me, leaned into me and kissed me on the forehead. 'How are you, love?' Her voice embraced me, covered me like a protecting cloak. 'It's good to see you, Danny.'

Three hours earlier, I'd been charged with murder and it had occurred to me, after she'd been led away, crying, that she wouldn't come back again. I was dumbstruck with happiness to see her, to feel her touch, to breathe in her scent, to know that after everything, and in spite of everything, she still loved me as much as I still loved her.

'Mum, I'm so glad to see you!' I folded my arms around her for a moment and looked right at her. 'Mum, I'm sorry. I've not done any—'

'Don't worry.'

'Danny!' Dad's voice fell like a shadow. 'Danny, what the hell's happened here?'

He sat on the other side of the bed to Mum and looked directly at me, his face set, his body stiff with tension, his manner formal and accusing.

I returned his gaze and wondered how many other fifteen-year-olds he'd stared at like this, trying to get them to spill the gravy on their role in some dead dumb crime or other.

'Look at me, Danny!' I could feel his fingers drumming out an uneasy beat on the bed, his eyes seeking out the innermost workings of my mind. 'Danny, look at me!'

'Shut up, Jim!' Mum hissed at him.

He rose from the bed and folded his arms. 'All I want is an explanation. An explanation of the facts here. That's all. I'm entitled to that at least.'

I turned my head away so that I couldn't see him. I fixed my eyes on Mum and pretended he wasn't there. I tried to smile at Mum and wished Dad was in France, anywhere other than here, breathing down my neck and filling the room with the weight of his disappointment.

'Mum, when I tried to phone him . . .'

'Who?' she asked.

'Dad.'

'You're talking as if I wasn't here!' he barged in.

'I tried to phone him from the service station where I was arrested. Something really weird happened. *She* answered the phone . . .'

'She? Pascale?' Dad fired the words at me like rockets. 'What'd she say, Danny?'

I turned on him and hissed, 'Why don't you just piss off back to Paris and find out for yourself?' He looked shocked, shocked to the core and offended with it. I hung onto his gaze with my eyes, wide and defiant, waiting for him to respond which he did after what seemed a long, long time.

'Don't you want me here? Is that it, Danny? Do you want me to leave? I'm your dad, Danny.'

'You don't have to be here, Dad. You left us, remember, for a different life. I was a disappointment to you, remember, and Mum just wasn't good enough . . .'

He opened his mouth to speak and slowly closed it.

'Go home, Dad, this doesn't involve you. Go back to Pascale, that's your home now.'

'Danny, please, listen to me. It wasn't like that. It wasn't against you or your mother, it wasn't like that at all. What have I done? What have I done wrong? I fell in love, that's all. I've come all the way from Paris to try and help you out and you're talking to me like this. Look at me, Danny, when I'm speaking to you, look at me.'

It was hard but I made myself keep looking at him, and as his face grew redder I noticed there was more grey hair around his ears and less on his scalp than there used to be. His widow's peak was sharper than I remembered and he needed a shave. Forty-eight hours ago, I thought this man knew most of the answers to any question worth asking. There was a hint of nicotine on his front teeth and a deep furrow across the top of his nose, between his eyes. My memory of him, and the image of the man who sat on my bed, were two different creatures altogether. A single shiver of embarrassment doused my spine. This man on the bed, with unwanted tears in the waxy whites of his eyes, this man was my father.

'Danny, why are you talking to me like this?' He looked and sounded insecure, confused, wrapped up in his own feelings.

He stood up and turned this way and that, a weak and selfish man searching around desperately, in a small room, for a place to hide which just wasn't there. He looked at Mum and pleaded, 'Tell him, Jenny! Tell him.'

'Tell him what?'

'You haven't changed, have you, Dad? I've been charged with murder. I'm innocent but I've been accused of killing a child, I've been accused of the worst thing imaginable and my life's over before it had a chance to start. And all you want to talk about's you and the way you feel and how it reflects on you. I don't give a toss about your finer feelings, Dad. In fact, I'll be honest, you're the biggest letdown in this family. Not me. Not Mum. You, Dad, you and your broken promises and your lies and your big talk and your selfish face.'

'Don't say this, Danny . . .'

'You abandoned me, you miserable bastard! What do you want me to say?'

'Then, I'd better go,' he said. And within a moment, he walked away again. He stopped at the door, his primal instinct to always have the last word, forcing him to call, 'Danny! Just you wait till you get to my age. Then you'll understand . . .' He swam against the cold current of his own most profound shame.

'Dad, when I get to your age, if I'm lucky, Dad, and very well behaved, Dad, they might be releasing me from jail . . . Dad!'

He didn't look directly at me, he just closed the door softly and was gone.

'Danny, are you OK?' asked Mum, touching my forehead. 'You're hot!'

'I was trying to tell you, Mum, about the call to Paris. Pascale told me I was *dead*, Mum! Dead? I just don't get it.'

'Well, Danny, yes, that's right . . .'

'Mum, what do you mean, that's right?'

'You phoned me, son, you told me you'd taken a whole bottle of sleeping tablets, that you were going to die, and hung up! I dialled the operator to find out where you'd called from. A public payphone in Oxford.'

'That wasn't me, Mum.'

'But, Danny, I know your voice. I am your mother.'

'It was Richard Pike. He can mimic anyone to perfection. He phoned you up and pretended to be me and told you that I'd taken the tablets. I didn't know he'd said that. He told me he'd called you to let you know I was OK. He was lying to me and torturing you.'

'Why?' she asked, her face perplexed, her voice amazed. 'Why?'

'Because he can. Because he's like that. Because he enjoys the suffering he inflicts on other people. But he seemed so decent, so kind . . . I'm sorry, Mum.'

'Don't be sorry, Danny.'

'But I am sorry for running off on you and the mean letter I left you and the worry I've caused and the trouble I'm in.'

'Danny, I don't really know what's happened to you in the last seven days but I do know that you wouldn't really do anything to hurt anyone.'

Outside, the daylight was fading and a warm orange sunset was forming in the sky; a dust of golden light fell around the room, blurring the sharper edges of everything around us, mixing shadows with silence and casting what felt like an invisible veil around Mum and me. In those few moments, I was away from all my troubles.

Mum looked up to the window where the light was seeping in and smiled in a way that I'd almost forgotten she could smile.

'You know, Danny, strange as it may seem, this is the happiest day of my life.'

'Why?'

'Because you're still here and you're still alive. I thought I'd lost you, I was getting ready to bury you, but . . .' She looked at me, smiling past herself, and touched my face.

'You're still here, lad, you're alive, and that's why this is the best day I've ever known.'

'You forgive me?' I asked.

'There's nothing to forgive, Danny. You've done nothing wrong.'

23

Killer

I lay perfectly still in the bed, wide awake, watching the moon through the window and floating in a numbness close to rigor mortis, unconnected memories escaping from the back of my memory like vapours from a poisoned wishing well.

I was back in Junior School, legs crossed on the wooden floor of the hall, listening to the Head Teacher telling a story with a meaning.

'*There was once a man who lived in a house at the bottom of a hill, on top of which was a massive boulder. Every day when he came home from work, he dreaded finding the boulder having rolled down the hill and flattened his house. Until the day came when it finally happened. Did he pull his hair out and scream? No. Instead, he blew the heaviest sigh of relief. The worst thing imaginable, the thing he dreaded most had really happened . . .*'

The worst thing they could accuse me of, the worst thing had been said, the unthinkable had happened to me and the man in the story, with the smashed up house, was clearly insane.

I wanted to shrink to something less than the ground-in gum on the police station floor, to vanish from sight and never be remembered again but, I knew, that was the last thing that was about to happen to me.

Ian Brady and Myra Hindley, Frederick and Rosemary West, Richard Pike and Daniel Anderson . . . Daniel Anderson? Oh, that Daniel Anderson, the child murderer. Hope he rots in hell . . . Mind you, he'll not see the light of day again, still, if you ask me, it's a waste of taxpayers' money keeping him locked up and alive inside some luxury prison or other when really he should hang for what he did!

This was it, the things in people's hearts and minds, the words that would pour from their mouths on buses and supermarkets, ordinary, decent, law-abiding men and women on the street, the men and women set to be picked for jury service.

It was this that was about to happen to me. This.

★ ★ ★

The following morning, Mr Emlyn Jones, a barrister, arrived to see me and stayed for over three hours. When he entered the room it was like a theatrical event, his head and shoulders towering over the guard who escorted him in, his width just about squeezing through the doorway, Miss Kerr following him like a page boy in a pantomime. His black suit was immaculate and in his movements, in spite of his size, he had the grace and style of a ballet dancer. Without being asked, without thinking, without speaking, I got up from the bed and stood upright, forgetting my back pain, hands at my side, eyes ahead, head back. There was something about Mr Emlyn Jones that made me want to do this soldier-like thing, this standing to attention. Natural authority flowed from him like water from a tap.

He picked up a chair with one hand and swung his briefcase onto the bed with the other. 'Get back into bed, Danny, you're ill!'

I obeyed immediately and watched him peering at me from a short distance, eyeing me up, seeing what I was like. Miss Kerr sat on the bottom edge of the bed and was clearly in awe of him; she watched him like Weasel's followers watched Weasel, like he was a movie star. She introduced us and he snared my hand in his, shaking it as if he was testing a tree for any rotten fruit.

'Seeing as your mum's in the unfortunate position of being on income support, the taxpayer's footing the bill for my services, Danny, so that means every moment you spend being anything less than one hundred per cent honest with me's not only a waste of time, it's a waste of money and that's just not on. You understand?' His voice was deep, musical and had a gravelled edge, a voice somewhere between poetry and song, a voice that swept you along in its rhythm and character.

'I understand. No lies.'

He breathed in supreme confidence and breathed out raw charisma.

'Are you Welsh?' he asked.

'No, I'm a Liverpudlian. My gran, she was from Wales.'

'I know, your mother told me . . . Your mum, she's convinced you're innocent. Is she right or is she just blinkered about her child?'

'She's right.'

'One hundered per cent right?'

'One hundred per cent. No lies, Mr Jones, I swear to God . . .'

'And I've read the brief, your account of things as told to Miss Kerr . . . Looks to me like you've been stitched up like a Christmas turkey . . .' He snapped open his case with, 'Then we have a basis from which we can act in your favour. The thing is, do you want me to represent you?'

'Yes, I do.'

'OK, there are two things I want to talk about. One's a question, one's a warning. Question first. Did you see this Pike character burning the jackets?'

'No. There was just a charred mass on the ground . . .'

'So, he could have burned his own jacket and planted your jacket at the scene of the murder?'

'Yeah, he could have done that, easily . . .'

Mr Jones made a note on his pad and muttered, 'That's fine, that's fine . . .' and looked up at me. 'Ready for the warning shot?' I nodded and knew, more or less, what was coming next.

'The rave,' I sighed.

'He's made a confession of sorts. He's admitted being an accessory after the fact to a second murder . . .'

'Well, what does that mean? There was another killing?'

'At Chipping Norton, the night you went to the rave. A seventeen-year-old girl called Kathy.' Miss Kerr spoke very evenly.

'We gave her a lift there, her and her friends . . .' I told them.

'I know,' Mr Jones replied.

'What happened to her?'

'She was kicked to death in a field outside the marquee,' Miss Kerr said.

The news sank into my brain like acid into polystyrene, burning where it touched. 'He killed Kathy?' I could smell her blood, feel it clinging to my skin. He stood tall in my memory, soaked to the skin in blood, with his tale of being attacked by three lads. My mouth was flooded with the taste of blood; I had accidentally bitten down on my tongue.

'What's his story then?' I asked.

'You went missing with Kathy . . .' Miss Kerr handed me a handkerchief. 'He went looking for you . . .'

'Don't tell me,' I interrupted. 'And he came across me kicking the life out of her and tried to stop me but it was too late!'

'Yes,' confirmed Mr Jones. 'That's about the top and bottom of it.'

'I was nowhere near the rave. I left early, went for a drive, fell asleep . . .'

'Anyone see you?' asked Mr Jones.

I shook my head and sighed, 'No.'

'Go over this with me again and if there's anything you haven't told us, anything you've forgotten, then make a note and we'll add it in. Begin.'

I focused on the opening line and read, 'On Monday 13th March, following a lot of rows at home with my mother, I decided to leave home.'

24

Taggart Hall

Taggart Hall was built by a rich Victorian merchant who'd wanted to impress his friends and enemies alike with his wealth. When he finally died, in 1863, when he wanted to impress God, and he couldn't take the house or money with him, the Hall was left to the poor children of Oxfordshire. A hundred and forty plus years down the line, it was home to the younger joyriders, arsonists and robbers of the Thames Valley area and, because it had a locked-up, secure unit attached to the main house, was to be my home also.

I arrived during the early hours of the morning so that the other teenagers who'd found themselves stuck there wouldn't be sent into hyper-space by the spectacle of my arrival.

It was a massive place, with towers and arches, a house trying to be a castle, with a driveway long enough to lay twenty full size football pitches down end to end. With the moon hanging low in the sky, the place looked like something from an old Hammer horror film, bathed in a cocktail of silver light and the aching shadows of the tall trees that were spread throughout the grounds leading up to the front door.

Tom, a silver-haired residential social worker, with the look and manner of a regimental Sergeant Major, sat next to me in the back of the unmarked police car, explaining it all away.

'Of course, you're going to a secure unit. You won't have the freedom to come and go like the other kids but you didn't expect anything different, did you?'

'No!'

'You're still a child, in the eyes of the law, that's how as you avoided going to a young offender institute. Lucky for you.'

As we made our way to the main door at the front of the house, Tom held onto my elbow in a grip that could have turned chalk to dust. I tried not to betray the pain I was in when I pointed at his blanched knuckles and said, 'Tom, I'm not going to do a runner.'

He looked about, there were two plainclothes officers following us. He relaxed his grip just enough to allow the blood to flow through my veins and we passed across the cavernous hall to a wide, dark doorway.

There was a security panel on the door frame, through which Tom swiped an ID card and tapped in a twelve-digit code with impressive speed. He then pulled out a long mortice key which he fitted into a lock set deep into the door's body. 'Home sweet home,' he said, pushing it open. He switched on a light and the cops followed us as we passed a row of locked doors, each with their own peepholes which told me the bottom line, I was back in the cells again.

'The rooms are all pretty much of a muchness,' he told me as he opened the last door on the corridor. 'A bed, a basin, a toilet, a table and chair . . . Do you like your own company?' he asked, rather suddenly.

'I guess so,' I replied, wandering into the room.

'Just as well,' Tom informed me. 'You'll be spending a lot of time on your own here. You're innocent till proved guilty, so you can have visitors whenever you like, so long as it isn't three in the morning. Mail, newspapers, whatever your family and friends want to send you, so long as it isn't illegal.'

'There's no one else on the unit then?' I asked. Tom shook his head and nodded towards the bed.

'Goodnight!' He hit the light and closed the door before I had a chance to turn around and reply, locking me up for the night.

The moonlight kissed the barred window and turned the room into a gathering place where ghosts came to end their earthly wanderings. I sat down on the floor and listened for the silent rattling of their imaginary chains, and, all of a sudden, felt that my sanity was balanced on nothing broader than the edge of a penny piece. Somewhere near the window, a central heating pipe groaned and echoed, and sounded like Richard Pike laughing out loud at me.

I stood up, as tall as I could, turned to the window and, fists clenched at my sides, laughed right back – loud and hard – until the noise died out and the room settled down to quietness.

I kicked off my trainers – I was still without laces – and climbed, fully dressed, under the cool quilt. As sleep picked at the stitching of my overheated brain, and the moon shifted her position in the sky, I sensed three long thin shadows fall from the bars on the window across my face.

There are no ghosts, I told myself, *not even ghosts would gather here!*

★ ★ ★

'For the benefit of the tape,' said Parker, 'DCI Waites is showing Daniel Anderson a handwritten confession from Richard Pike in which he admits to knowing of the death of Kathy Hewlett and that he witnessed the accused, Daniel Anderson, kicking her repeatedly about the head, injuries which caused her to die. Read it, Daniel.'

I took my time, read over the fabrications and handed it back.

During the rave, Daniel said to me, 'Let's teach the bitch a lesson she won't forget!' He meant Kathy who we'd given a lift to. We were both high on speed and had been drinking. I told him to drop it and he went off in a nark. But I noticed he was nowhere to be seen and Kathy was missing also. I went to the exit and saw them walking to the field where she died. So I followed but lost them because it was dark. I carried on, calling after them and heard a cry. I followed the noise and he was kicking her and hitting her with a rock. By the time I got there it was too late. He had killed her. Daniel murdered Kathy. I realise I am guilty of not telling the police and, in this, for protecting him, am in the wrong and deserve to be punished for this.

'Why did you do it, Daniel?'

'I didn't do anything. He's a liar!' I said, calmly.

'Daniel,' said Waites, 'we've got statements from two girls, Kathy's friend and Kathy's cousin, Laura, and Jayne. They described you as acting weirdly. They saw you taking drugs. *You* tried to make *them* take drugs.'

'They said you took drugs in the toilet at the Little Chef, you were *"gone for ages and came out nearly delirious"*. Jayne said that.'

I said nothing.

'Why did you do it, Daniel?' Waites wanted to know.

'Did she laugh at you?' Parker enquired.

'Were you high on speed? Is that why?' Waites persisted.

'I'm sorry, I don't think there's any more point in answering your questions,' I replied. 'You won't listen to me!' I sat back in my seat and eyeballed them.

'Why don't *you* give *us* a break,' said Waites. 'Tell us the truth for a change.'

'I've told the truth all along and you don't believe me,' I said. 'I've nothing else to say.'

'I'm going to do you a favour, Daniel,' said Parker. 'I'm going to warn you. Nowadays, this sort of deliberate silence is looked on by the courts as an admission of guilt. Do you understand? You're hurting no one but yourself.'

'OK!' I lurched forward. 'He's laughing at all of you, at all of us!'

'What do you mean?'

'When he killed Kathy, I was miles away. I left the rave and went for a drive.'

'But, Daniel, we've got forensic evidence. We've got traces of Kathy's blood on your clothes.'

'Richard came up to me and embraced me, that's how her blood came onto me. He told me a cock and bull tale about being in a fight with three lads. We went and washed in a stream.'

'That doesn't seem credible,' said Parker. 'That doesn't seem at all likely.'

'Daniel,' continued Waites, 'you don't really expect us to accept that? Do you?'

'We'll take a break,' said Parker, 'just for a minute or two.' They sent for tea and went into a huddle in the corner, out of earshot.

I turned to Miss Kerr and Mum, and held my hands up, feeling the weight of defeat like a dead weight around my head, neck and shoulders.

'Mum, I think I'm going mad.'

'No you're not, Danny. You're down on your luck, life will change, it must.'

'Just be patient,' said Miss Kerr. 'Don't do or say anything silly. Co-operate.'

'OK!' said Parker. 'Recommencing interview . . . 12.25 pm . . . Same persons present as earlier . .' Waites sat down and faced me.

'Danny,' he sighed, 'we know you had a motive for attacking Kathy.'

'Fox hunting!' Parker announced. 'You hated her

because she took part in the hunt. That's why you killed her . . . because you value animal life above human life.'

'Wrong,' I whistled into the wind.

'Do you know a Mrs Sarah Blackwell, Danny?' asked Parker.

'No, never heard of her.'

'She knows you. She's the owner of The White Stag, the hotel you stayed in the night before the fox hunt. She's made a statement, she said she heard you say, and I quote, *I'd like to get a couple of redcoats and crack their skulls open!* Did you say that?'

'Yes, I did . . . but I didn't mean it. It was just talk.'

'You got your wish, Danny. You certainly cracked open a couple of skulls . . .' Parker sounded deeply unhappy, but looked like the cat with her paw on the mouse's back.

'We've got forensic evidence, a motive and a witness who heard you say what you'd like to do before you did it.' Waites was almost giving me mouth to mouth resuscitation, breathing into my eyes and ears.

Parker stood up and said, 'Daniel Anderson, on Saturday 18th March, at Chipping Norton in the County of Oxford, I am charging you with the murder of Kathy Hewlett . . .'

Waites formally terminated the interview and turned off the tape, handing one copy to Miss Kerr and slipping the other into a brown envelope for their side.

'OK! No more questions, for now. Go back to Taggart Hall!'

25

Love Letters

I was eating scrambled eggs and toast at my table when Tom knocked on the door and called, 'Are you busy, lover boy?'

I laid my knife and fork down and turned to the door. 'Come in, Tom!'

His usual stony face was cracked with mirth lines and, in his hands, he carried a small bundle of envelopes, the waft of cheap perfume sailing across the room as he waved them in the air, with, 'Cupid's here!'

'What's this?'

'You're famous now.'

'No, I'm not. They can't crack on in the papers who I am, or print my picture. I'm too young to be identified . . . Mr Jones said so!'

'Oh, Danny,' Tom laughed. 'This is the modern world!' He threw the bundle down on the bed. My name and current address were on the top envelope in what looked like female handwriting. 'You're a celebrity, old son,' Tom told me. 'They can't say anything about you in the press but there are seven websites on the Internet about you!'

'You're kidding!' I replied.

'No, God's honour, there are pictures of you and information about you all over the Net.'

'Pictures? Which pictures?'

'I don't know, I'm not linked to the Net.'

Suddenly, I lost all interest in my breakfast but tried not to show too much interest in the bundle on my bed. Tom hovered in the doorway.

'Yes, Tom?'

'Aren't you going to open them?'

'No,' I said, turning back to my food. 'I'm going to finish my breakfast.'

As soon as he closed the door after himself, I turned and sat down with the pile on the bed. I spread out the envelopes, they were all the same colour, white, and same size, A3, with the same postmark, Hastings, posted on the same date, Thurs Aug 1, with the same neat joined-up handwriting in vivid purple fountain pen. Each envelope was numbered in the top left-hand corner with a number from 1 to 13 in order. I teased open the flap of letter number 1, pulled out the white, unlined paper and read the precise handwriting:

17 Vaughan Crescent,
Hastings,
East Sussex,
HR1 1RH.

1st August, Thursday.

Dear Danny,
I understand. Let me make that perfectly clear to you at the outset of our relationship. I understand the pressures and

problems that drove you to take the life of an innocent child, and let me also make it clear to you that I do not condemn you for this or for anything or for any action no, quite the opposite. In fact. If you are guilty that is which is not clear till you are proved so in a court of law, you did do it didn't you, my Danny?!!?! (You are big star on the internet, my love) The thing is, I love you. As soon as I saw your picture on the screen, dressed in that smart velvet jacket, I fell hopelessly head over heels in love with you, Danny. Danny, Danny, Danny, I say the word, how sweet it is to me like music to my poor ears. I want to visit you soon, I must see you to make my feelings certain, to show you I love you with my whole mind, and heart, and body, because in a letter like this it is one thing and that is fine and I love you madly but there is a distance between us that only meeting can bridge. I will stand by you throughout this and will wait faithfully for you throughout, and when you are sixteen, on your birthday, we can get married and have children of our own, I know you would be a good father, I can see it in your eyes, you are a kind young man. My name is Juliet Morrissey, I am 21 years old and live here at home with my Mum. I am a model and enclose a photograph of me taken recently on my last modelling job. I am going to give up modelling to make a home for us so say you love me Danny, say it please, write to me and tell me by next post, and say we will meet, Danny, don't let me down, I beg you, or I will die of sadness. I love you all the world, get linked to the Net.

Juliet

xxxxxxxxxxxxxxxxxxxxxxxxxxxxxxxxxxxxxxxxxxxxxxx

There was a folded page, torn from a magazine in the envelope, taken from *Hello!* magazine, a picture of the Wonderbra girl. So, this was Juliet?

I opened letter number two and read more of the same and by the end of number five I stopped. I decided I'd had enough, I had a headache.

26

Happy Birthday, Sweet Sixteen

'You've got a visitor,' said Tom, pushing the door open to let them in.

'Mum!' Without thinking, I jumped up from the bed and went towards the door to meet her. Instead, Dad appeared in the doorway, carrying a large brown cardboard box and wearing the sort of fixed grin that would have looked forced in a silent movie.

'Dad,' I said, trying to mask my disappointment at not seeing Mum, and my shock at seeing him. 'Come in, Dad!' The box read: *Sharp 14" Colour Portable Television*.

'Happy birthday, son!' He placed the box on the table and said, 'Open it up!' He took my hand and gave it a strong, manly shake, before I could wriggle free and set about undoing the box. 'You seemed surprised to see me?'

'I was a bit. Thanks for your card.'

'I bet you were thinking, *Hey, where's the money?*'

'No, not really. I'm not in the position to go browsing down the shops.'

I lifted the TV out and found the remote control. The TV was matte black and had a silver, circular, indoor aerial on top. 'Thanks a lot, Dad.'

'It's the least I can do.' I didn't argue the point.

'Are you pleased to see me?'

'Yes, Dad, I'm pleased to see you.'

'Has your mother told you I'm back in Liverpool, permanently now.'

'Yes, she said.'

'Living at your Auntie Mae's.'

'How is Auntie Mae?'

'She's . . . well, she's not really taken it very well . . . y'know, the way things have turned out.'

'She always was a self-pitying cow.' He buckled and frowned but I carried right on. 'Sorry, Dad, I know she's your sister but I don't feel obliged to keep my feelings in any more.'

He forced what I took to be a wise smile. 'Well, if a son can't level with his dad . . .' he began, so I changed the subject immediately.

'Mum tells me you're working.'

As Dad started filling me in on his life, I noticed his clothes and, in particular, his jacket. It was brand new, a pastel shade of purple, a middle-aged man's copping-off jacket that matched the natural highlights of his face. It was a real baddie, the sort of garment that screamed out loud about the wearer, *I've got no taste in clothes but think I'm a born again trendsetting dandy!*

'Is there something wrong with this jacket?' asked Dad, pausing in mid-flow.

'No . . . no . . .'

'You keep looking at it and frowning?'

'Carry on, Dad,' I told him, and imagined him in a bar somewhere, chatting up a woman, any woman, probably someone dead young, and not very fussy and totally flaky.

His tie matched the jacket and was flecked with tiny white dots. I wondered what lies he'd hit her with, and if the mid-life philandering gene was in me.

'Like I was saying,' he continued. 'I'm working for a security company, as a guard, but that's just for now. The supervisor reckons, with my experience, it won't be long before I'm on my way up to better things.'

'Good, I'm happy for you.'

'I'm based in the Clayton Square shopping centre. I won't be a security guard for long . . .'

'Dad, what do you want?'

'I've come to see you, Danny, it's your birthday.'

'I know. But I get the feeling you want to ask me something.'

'No, Danny!' His voice was firm but I could tell by his eyes he was dithering.

He straightened up and looked about the room. For better or worse, I could tell, the subject was about to change again, dramatically. He pulled a pack of Silk Cut from his pocket and, just before he lit up, paused and asked, 'May I?' He lit up.

'Danny? What do you know about Richard Pike?'

'Very little,' I replied. 'And what he did tell me was a bundle of lies. Why do you ask?'

'I'm still in touch with some of the blokes on the force. It's just . . . he's a complete and utter mystery. I wondered if you knew anything.'

'I've told Miss Kerr and Mr Jones absolutely everything I know. Why do want to know?'

'It's this stuff in the papers, this Invisible Man business . . .'

'Oh, Dad, it's a name made up to sell newspapers!' I cut him off and I was on my feet and pacing, but he carried on.

'You know he told the investigating officers his name was Richard Pike; they also had to hand the fact he'd told you his name was Luke Frears but there's no record of him, or if there is they can't find it. There's no medical records, no school records, no national insurance number, no social security, no bank or building society account, no driver's licence, no credit . . . it's like he's never existed.'

I'd avoided the newspapers like a plague of boils but I'd heard all these whispers and rumours from Miss Kerr and Mr Jones.

'Unless Pike's a false name,' I suggested. 'Does he have blood in his veins? Is it green or red, Dad?'

'Blood type O positive . . . They've trawled the missing persons register, no joy. He's got no dental records, his fingerprints don't match any on file . . . They showed his photo to every family in the UK with a missing son between the ages of sixteen and twenty-four and not one stepped forward to claim him.'

'Maybe somebody doesn't want him!'

'Maybe so, Danny. But, so far, it's like he's literally come out of nowhere.'

'How's he been, with the coppers and prison officers?'

'Polite but in denial of ever having a family, being at school or having a life. He says he can't remember a thing up to the moment he met you. His memory's very clear from that point on. He can't even remember where he got the Range Rover. Did he tell you where he got the money?'

'Yeah, Dad, he told me a heartbreaking story. The truth? He probably stole it. Has it turned up yet?' I asked, anticipating the answer.

'No. No sign, no trace.'

Dad squashed his cigarette out in the sink where I washed my face and poured himself a beaker of water.

'He's laughing at them,' I said, feeling a chill that grew colder by the moment as Dad had succeeded in reminding me of the non-person smokescreen that Pike had thrown up around himself and the gaudy myths that were growing up around him. 'He'd be laughing his face to shreds if he heard us sitting here like a pair of geeks having this conversation. You want to know what I think, Dad? About Pike? I think he's from some ordinary little house in some boring little town, some dull and narrow street, some shabby little family with its nasty little secrets and its grubby little appetites. That's what I think. Zip. End of story.'

'Danny, they put his picture up on "Crimewatch". Eight million viewers and . . .' He clicked his fingers. 'That response. Not one phone call, not even a crank call.'

'What about his signature in the guest books of the hotels?'

'He printed his name and the address he gave just doesn't exist, not even anything like it. It's like, he's . . .'

Dad lit another and drew down deep on his fag while he looked for the right words. 'It's like he's a bogeyman!'

'Dad, you know, I just can't believe you're buying this garbage.'

'I'm just repeating what I've heard.'

'Well, let me assure you, he eats, drinks, sleeps and goes to the toilet.'

'I know, I'm just . . .'

'What used you to say to me? Give me the facts and leave the flim-flam in the pedal bin.'

'Danny, I'm trying hard to get to grips with the facts.'

'OK, Dad,' I calmly announced. 'I'll give you a fact to get to grips with. And the fact is he's running rings round the system, round the cops, round the media, round everyone who's dumb enough to buy his story. He's not a superior intelligence and he didn't arrive on a spaceship. But the thing is it's a tough act to keep up, this selective amnesia business, and sooner or later, his luck'll run out. He'll trip himself up. And all the people who went around scratching their chins and speculating'll be denying that they were ever taken in by it all. You'll see.'

'D'you like the telly?' he said, suddenly changing the subject.

'Yeah, yes I do, thanks, Dad!'

For all my tough talk though, the whole Invisible Man palaver unnerved me, made strange noises go off in the dark part of my brain, noises that reverberated all around the underside of my skin, setting me out in goose pimples. It conjured a dire panic, like a part of me was drowning while the rest of me sat hopelessly paralysed, unable to do anything but watch.

'I put the plug on. I guessed you wouldn't have a screwdriver handy!'

'You guessed right.'

'Are you cold?' he asked. 'You're shivering.'

'Summer cold,' I replied.

'Cooped up in the central heating,' he muttered, taking his jacket off, and revealing a damp circle around his armpit.

Dad switched the TV on and flicked around the channels, adjusting the indoor aerial to get the clearest reception. 'Well, it's a good picture,' he said, as the credits on the end of 'Neighbours' rolled by, and then, in the same breath, he told me, 'Danny, there is something else.' He turned and looked down at me. He smiled and looked straight into my eyes. I was right all along. He did want something for himself and now we were going to talk bald turkey.

'What do you want, Dad?'

'Danny, I'll be the first to admit, I've been a first-rate fool, walking out on you and your mother, throwing it all away for . . .' He couldn't say her name now. Strangely enough. But I could. 'Pascale,' I whispered, remembering the time I saw her in her black swimsuit. He half-frowned and skated past her name and memory. 'There's no way I can reverse time and undo the damage I've done . . . but I can try and make the future better. I'll be blunt. I want to go home. I want to move back in with your mum and try again.'

'So, ask her!' Such was life for him at Auntie Mae's. The thought amused me and I had to hide a smile.

'I have done . . . she's been hurt, I'm guilty of that, and she's being rather hard to get through to . . .'

'You want me to put a good word in for you?'

'You're a mind reader, son, you must be psychic.'

'I'll do what I can for you.'

'Danny, I'd really appreciate it.'

'I can't promise it'll do any good. Like you say, she's been hurt, but I'll try.'

Our conversation walked abruptly into a stone wall of silence and knocked itself out. I caught him taking a sly look at his wristwatch.

'Danny, I've got to get back to Liverpool. I've things to do, y'know how it is.'

'Of course.' The relief that the visit was coming to a close was mutual and we were both on our feet, shaking hands, double quick, like a father and son in a Gillette advert.

His aim accomplished, he was gone. I flicked through the channels till I came across an advert for chewing gum with a bright jingle which I sang along with as loud as I could, while I jumped to my feet and danced wildly and unhappily around the room.

'You can't beat the pleasure, you can't beat the fun,
Of Hubba Wubba, Hubba Wubba Bubble Gum!'

★ ★ ★

'We've got a date for court, Danny.' Mr Jones dropped the news casually, too casually, like he was telling me he'd just remembered how he'd bought a pair of brown bootlaces only the other day. He produced a letter and handed it to me.

I'd found myself growing ultra-receptive to tones of voice of late, an avid and eager reader of tiny facial expressions and interpreter of minor mood swings. Kerr and Jones were making the nerves in my teeth buzz so I turned from them and opened the letter out, my eyes weaving straight through the body of print to the vital details, *Thursday, 31st October, 10 am.* 'That's quite quick,' he told me. 'Sometimes you can wait nine months, a year, more than a year; with this, they're steaming it through.'

That's because they've got me, I thought. 'October 31st? Halloween? At least there'll be no more waiting around. At least we'll know the worst,' I was thinking out loud. 'Halloween, when the evil spirits walk the earth . . .'

'Halloween, you're not superstitious, are you?'

'No,' I replied. 'But they only push cases forward to court this quickly when it's a dead cert conviction. Dad always used to say that.'

'That's right, Danny,' Jones had to agree. 'But remember, there's two of you going in the dock. We have to go in believing that the certain conviction's going to be Pike!'

'Me versus the Invisible Man?' I now understood the reason why I was picking up the offbeat vibration from my legal team. The early date was the kiss of death to my fragile dreams of freedom.

Kerr jumped in, 'You're not guilty, so don't think guilty, don't talk guilty, and don't act guilty!'

I then noticed the way they were watching me and the way they were looking at each other. They were eyeing one another out to see who'd be the first to speak.

'I think,' Jones announced quietly, 'you've been through a great deal of stress.' I sat down on the bed. I was in control. I was listening carefully. Miss Kerr sat beside me on the bed and pressed one of my hands between two of hers. 'You've had a lousy time of it and we're a little bit worried . . .'

'I'm sixteen, my name is Daniel, the earth revolves around the sun, two plus two makes four, I'm in the most trouble it's humanly possible to be in and it looks like I'm going to spend the rest of my life locked up, I'm scared, I'm very scared, in fact, but I'm not mad!'

Jones was firm but quiet. 'We don't think you're a hopeless psychiatric case. But we'd be lying if we said we weren't worried.'

'So, how long have you been worried about me?' All the times they came to see me, as soon as they closed the door, they must have been swopping notes. *How do you think he's doing? Did you see his face twitch when the watch alarm went off?*

'We worry about how you'll do in court. We have to face up to reality, before we finally get there. You're going to have to sit in the dock with Pike and face all manner of questions. We can try for a postponment. We can get a doctor to see you.'

'But I don't want that.'

'Why, Danny?' Miss Kerr tried to engage my eyes with hers.

'Why? Because you only need a doctor when you're sick. I saw a tribe of psychiatrists between March and May and got the all-clear, remember? Is Pike seeing a shrink?'

'Pike is . . . yeah, most definitely!' replied Mr Jones.

'Yeah, that's because he's a bloody nutcase. I repeat. I'm not mad and I'm not guilty. What were you saying the other minute? I'm not guilty, don't think guilty, don't speak guilty, don't act guilty. And I'm not hiding. What's the point in putting it off? Why do you want to put it off a single moment longer than necessary?'

'All right, Danny. Point taken. No, I'm sure you'll be fine,' said Jones. 'October 31st it is. We'll have to sort a suit out for you.'

I looked to Miss Kerr, she shrugged and said, 'I'm sure you'll cope very well.'

As afternoon turned to dusk, when everyone'd gone, when the door was closed, when there was no one outside in the corridor, I walked to the window and, looking between the bars, watched my reflection in the glass and thought, Do they have a point?

The boyhood had left my face and there in its place was a quizzical young man looking directly back at me.

It was a difference I was sure no one else would notice. It was a difference no one else would care about.

'Are you just getting older?' I asked my reflection. 'Or am I getting old before my time?'

27

Halloween

Richard Pike had his back turned to me.

As I made my way towards the door that led up into the court, I saw him for the first time in over seven months. On either side, he was flanked by uniformed cops. I tried to deaden my footfall so he couldn't hear me, but the harder I tried to kill the sound of my steps, the louder they echoed around the bare tiled walls of the basement cells of Oxford Crown Court.

In half a step forward and less than the blink of an eye, I weighed myself up against him. He was wearing a very expensive suit, an uncreased black jacket, tailor-made, his shoulders wider than I remembered (like he'd been doing weights), his hair immaculately groomed, square necked, like he'd just walked from a poster on the barber's shop wall. I automatically reached for my hair, which was standing up at the back where I'd been lying on it. Mum and Dad had clubbed together and bought me a perfectly good blue suit, off the peg, from Next but one glance from the back told me he looked ten times better than I ever could. To look at, I was as good as I'd get and I looked and felt a mess.

I walked on, suddenly seized by two urges, one to rush forward and lay into the bastard with feet, fists and forehead and, then, to spin on the heels of my black leather shoes, break away from the coppers and run back into the cell. I walked on, taking deep breaths to calm the trembling that was rising up inside me as I came within metres of him and fancied I could smell his expensive aftershave.

I was about an arm's-length behind him when we finally stopped, and he turned his head three-quarters of a semi-circle. I could see one eye, the happy arch of his grinning mouth, his neatly defined jawline. How he smiled when I arrived, as if pleasantly surprised to see me, the very best of old friends. And he laughed. He laughed, quietly and confidently, and asked, 'Daniel, how are you?'

He sounded pleased to see me, genuinely happy that we were together again and it freaked me out. I stared back into his jet black pupil in the sea of blue iris and said, 'Richard Pike? Or do I still call you Luke?'

'How have they been treating you?' He looked me up and down. 'Nice suit, you're looking good,' he said, and then, 'I've been stuck in a young offender institute with arsonists and the like. Dreadful people.'

'OK, time!' The Clerk of the Court appeared in the doorway, addressed the policemen, didn't give either of us a second glance, and away we went.

'I was glad your name stayed out of the papers, and that you were placed in care. It's better than prison. I can tell you that for nothing. Are you OK, Daniel? They wouldn't let me write to you. That really pissed me off. You'll get life, you know, Daniel, you do realise that, don't you? I'm sorry but they'll send you away forever.'

We were marching up a spiral staircase now, two coppers between me and him, sandwiched between uniforms and led forwards by the black-cloaked Clerk.

'I know it's hard to talk just now, Daniel . . .'

'So shut up! Stop making noises with your mouth, *Richard*!'

'Don't be like that. Please. I promise you, Daniel, I'll write to you every week and come and see you once a month. I'll send you birthday cards and little decorations for your cell at Christmas. I'll still think of you when the rest of the world's forgotten what you looked like, when no one can quite remember your name!' So spoke Richard Pike, the kindest guy who ever lived, and I wondered why the guards didn't tell him to clam up, why they allowed him to do this to me. 'Have you missed me? Did you think about me when you were locked up?'

'Of course I did. I thought about you all the time, dressed up in a straitjacket and dreaming of Hitler and the Third Reich, and singing *Tomorrow Belongs to Me* like the Nazi scumbags in that old movie *Cabaret*. Of course I spared you a thought, you fifty pence shop Nazi. And, by the way, I worked it out, Richard, that all the money you spent on me, it came out of my building society book. You know, the one you stole from me, when you took my bag in the toilets . . . So, just for the record, I don't owe you a bean.'

'Daniel, why are you being like this?'

'Don't talk to me!'

'I'm not your enemy, Daniel.'

'All right, you two, cut the chatter out!' It was the Clerk of the Court, her name Eleanor Jane on the white ID card clipped to her jacket. She placed a finger across her lips and made a shushing sound to stress the point. She opened a wooden door and led us into the court room where an aching hush fell upon the packed rows in the public gallery and the eyes of the three teams of lawyers turned as we walked into the dock.

There was a choral gasp, a sound of curiosity that was aimed right at me for this was the first time they'd seen me. A woman whispered loudly, 'He doesn't look capable!' I did what the coppers told me and sat down in the dock, listening to the whispering and the sound of the jurors marching into their box. I faced the other way and saw Bowler Hat, and Sarah Blackwell from The White Stag. Laura and Jayne sat in front of Kyle's mum who was next to Weasel who held my gaze and raised a hand to his head, his fingers forming the barrel of a gun which he pressed to his temple and pulled back in recoil.

The public gallery was packed and, at first, I couldn't find Mum or Dad. They were on the back row, looking at me but looking through me, like I was a hologram. Mum smiled, but it dissolved before it had the chance to fully form.

'All stand!' the Clerk of the Court announced as the door to the judge's chambers opened. I stood up, my legs almost buckling under the weight of my body as Judge Andrew Warlock, in his red gown and white wig, began what was for him just another day at work.

With a flick of the hand, he indicated that we were

all to sit and spent the best party of a minute examining a document that was on his bench. He glanced up, looked directly at me and down at his document again.

Jones had told me to expect a three-cornered fight between him, the Crown Prosecution Service who wanted to send both of us away and Pike's barrister, Mr Saunders, who wanted Richard off and me to take the whole hodful.

'Mr Jones,' said Warlock. 'Any special petitions to make regarding the age of the accused?'

Jones stood up, looked at me and, turning back to Warlock, replied, 'No, M'Lord!'

'In that case,' said Warlock, his old and severe face forming into a creased mask of deep frowns, 'let's proceed with appointing the jury!'

★ ★ ★

'Ladies and gentlemen of the jury!' After all the weird and agonising scenes that had played themselves out in my head, concrete reality, with its long pauses, coughing and sneezing, shuffling papers and fidgeting onlookers, was here in the form of Mrs Deborah Murphy, barrister for the Crown Prosecution Service, whose job it was to send me and Pike away for life. She stood in front of the jury and began outlining her case against us.

'You've heard the charges against the accused and you've heard both of them plead not guilty on all counts – GBH, murder, accessory to murder, possession of an imitation firearm. You may have guessed, rightly, to use a rather old-fashioned expression, they've had the book thrown at them . . . and for good reason. *Why*? You may well ask. Quite simply, society can't afford not to throw everything at them. We can't allow these two on our streets. We intend to show that they're both guilty of all they've been charged with and their denial is the beginning of a long chain of downright lies!'

I could feel a real sense of darkness falling around me and a deeply painful pressure building in the core of my brain.

Murphy stopped, adjusted the glasses on her nose, then went on and took over an hour, lingering on details of how we'd stolen Kyle from his bed, used him as a human football and then carved him to shreds. How we'd lured Kathy out of the rave, with the intention of raping her but succeeded only in battering her so hard, mashing her head with rocks, that they found pieces of her brain thirty-five to forty metres from where she'd been slaughtered.

The jury watched and their mouths and jaws widened when they learned that Kyle had been kicked so hard that there was an imprint of *my* trainer sole on his back. One by one they turned their gaze from Murphy and across to me, their faces full of horror and disgust. I found myself looking back at them and through the spaces between their scandalised faces.

She indicated the dock with a wide sweep of the arm, pointing at each of us, without looking, and leaning into the jury, like she was going to share a rare and special secret with them.

'Ladies and gentlemen, Daniel Anderson and Richard Pike. You've heard the charges against them and the – very predictable – denials of guilt from both accused. Be warned. You're going to hear a lot more denial from both young men. You'll hear from each of them how it was the other who was responsible for the bloodshed and carnage that they caused in March of this year, when they went on an indiscriminate binge of murder for blind sadistic pleasure. Try not to wonder why these things happened, concentrate on the facts. Look past the lies, look at the evidence – the forensic evidence, the testimony of the witnesses, the video evidence. The Crown will prove beyond all reasonable doubt that Daniel Anderson and Richard Pike went out to murder or maim whoever was young enough or helpless enough or unfortunate enough to come into their sphere. *For a laugh!*'

She looked at us, for the first time, as she spoke these three final words. She stared at us, making the jury do the same; she walked a step or two in our direction, repeating, 'For a laugh!' And then, looking to Warlock, she returned to her bench, with a firm 'Thank you.'

Warlock was making notes, and didn't even look up when he announced, 'Mr Saunders.'

Saunders was getting on but had a thick head of blow-dried hair beneath his wig and a slick suit, that probably cost more than a good second-hand car. He gave out a strong vibration that he'd never known a moment of doubt in his entire life, he had a handle on truth, he was totally in the know. He smiled at the jury, his eyes stroking their faces, his eyes connecting with each of the twelve, one by one, drawing a smile here and a thaw out there. The jury liked Saunders and he hadn't even opened his mouth. And when he did, when they were all staring at him like little kids at a master storyteller, he said, 'Believe me, Richard Pike is a victim.'

I didn't know whether to laugh, cry or scream because all the instincts that drove me to do these three things welled up into one foul-tasting stew that jarred in my throat.

'Daniel!' I heard Richard speak my name clearly but I had the weird feeling that I was imagining the sound of his voice. I focused on Saunders, not wishing to give him the satisfaction of drawing my attention but again, 'Daniel!' he whispered, his slightly parted lips not moving, drawing my gaze into his space. It was like the voice wasn't coming out of him, it was a sound that drifted over me like a graveyard vapour and it made my skin tingle and the pores open up in a single second as if obeying a hidden order in his voice. Beads of sweat rolled down my neck and over the rollercoaster of my spine. 'Daniel, Daniel, Daniel!' His mouth was shut tight, his eyes fixed on his barrister, his voice as lucid as Saunders' but his lips sealed.

He took a white handkerchief from his pocket and handed it to me, 'You're sweating!' Now his words seemed to fall from the ether like a hail of invisible poisoned arrows. 'Listen to him,' Richard's voice commanded. 'Listen to what he's saying about you.' He wasn't even looking at me. A single shudder coursed through me. Somehow, he was speaking directly to my mind, passing messages with telepathy. His words seeped through my fingers. 'Listen to what he's saying about you, Mr Saunders, look how the jury are drinking his words in! I'm sorry, Daniel!'

Saunders looked like the jury's favourite uncle, as he told them, 'The video evidence will clearly prove that the first charge of GBH was entirely the responsibility of Anderson and Anderson alone . . .'

Softly, Richard laughed. I turned. He looked at me, he turned to face me for a moment and, speaking normally, asked simply, 'Yes?'

'Get out of my head!' I hissed.

The police guard shushed me and Pike just smiled and looked away as Warlock frowned, not sure if he'd quite heard a slight disturbance in his courtroom.

'The forensic evidence,' continued Saunders, 'the bloodstained suede jacket, the kitchen knife . . . the forensic evidence will prove beyond any reasonable doubt that the sole killer of Kyle Wolf was Daniel Anderson . . .'

Richard hissed. And hissed, and the policemen around us didn't move, didn't flicker, didn't appear to hear a thing. Richard hissed and stared at Saunders as he made his big theatrical progress before the jury; Richard's face was set, as the hissing grew louder, split into two distinct pitches, like a pair of alleycats squaring up for a midnight brawl. I was the only one who seemed to hear it.

'These crimes only involve Richard Pike because he was unfortunate enough to be in the wrong place at the wrong time. I will prove, however, that Daniel Anderson is guilty of all the charges laid before him by this court.'

Richard's head inclined slightly and he looked at me as Saunders headed back for his bench. He spoke, quite normally, 'I'm sorry, Daniel!'

Jones stood up to his full height, turned to the jury and as he opened his mouth to speak, to defend me, Warlock proclaimed, 'It's approaching 12.30, Mr Jones, it's been a long morning for the jury. We'll adjourn for lunch and come back at 2.15.'

Everyone stood up. The sides of my skull no longer felt strong enough to hold up the scrambled mess of my brain. As I watched Warlock leave the court, I felt my face seize up, twisted out of shape with rage. Richard looked at me, seriously, calmly, and said, 'Don't worry. We'll meet again!' I didn't answer, I was full. I was full of sorrow, anger, and despair that my mind felt buckled beyond repair. When the jury filed out, they couldn't even look across at me.

'I sing a new song now, a new hymn to the future,' Richard whispered. And he sang, *'We'll meet again . . . Don't know where, Don't know when . . . But I know we'll meet again some sunny day . . .'*

'What?'

We were corkscrewing our way down to the cells and he fell into a profound silence. He didn't even try to invade my unwilling head with his alien noise.

There were only footsteps on stone, their dying echo and the silent void into which they sank.

As they led him one way and me another, he turned his head, he smiled for a moment but there were real tears in his eyes.

28

You Wait, You Wonder

I refused to eat, I couldn't eat, I didn't want to eat. I refused to sit, I couldn't sit, I didn't want to sit. I was in a state of hypertension and all I wanted was to get back in there, to hear something good said about me, to hear my side of the story, that was all, not to hang about in the cells, thinking about the jury eating lunch while the phrase *first impressions mean the most* kept jumping out of nowhere. I waited at the the cell door, calling out to every passing set of feet.

'What's the time?'

'Two minutes later than last time.'

We'll meet again, Don't know where, Don't know when . . . I hated the song as it ramraided my head . . . *But I know we'll meet again . . .* Did I imagine him using telepathy in the dock? Was he singing in my head now? I felt utterly confused and when I heard Jones and Kerr heading my way, I cried out, 'Mr Jones, Miss Kerr, I'm just down here!'

Seeing them took the sharp edge from my desperation.

Kerr honed in on the untouched tray of food and said, 'You've got to eat!'

'I couldn't possibly.'

Jones pointed at the small bench that was fixed to the wall. 'I can't sit! I think Pike's throwing his voice, he keeps speaking to me and the guards don't seem to hear him.'

'Daniel, calm down, sit down!' Jones pulled me down beside him. 'The trial's been adjourned for the rest of the day.'

'What?'

'One of the jurors collapsed. Suspected epileptic fit!'

'You're joking!'

'No, Daniel, we're not joking. You'll have to go back to Taggart Hall and wait until Warlock calls us all back!'

'An epileptic fit? Are you sure?'

'Daniel, put your jacket on, we'll travel back with you.'

'An epileptic fit? Are you sure?'

★ ★ ★

When I got back, thirty-six hours had passed since I'd last slept. I spent the afternoon dozing on my bed and wishing I'd tumble into a dream dead sleep. But each time any peace came to me, I was nagged awake by a nail tapping my head, reminding me, *Don't go away because something's very wrong here!*

When Tom brought me my meal, I was sitting up and sleep was a lost horizon. A foody smell filled the room, the dense sweetness of tinned fruit, hot, fatty fresh fried chips and the cosmetic cheesy undercurrents of a micro-waved lasagne. I was empty but had no appetite whatsoever.

'You look tired,' said Tom as he placed the tray down. 'Try and get it while it's hot.'

'OK, Tom!' He lingered near the door.

'How'd it go?' he asked, at last. 'Did they outline the prosecution case?'

'Yeah.'

'How'd it come across?'

'Like I'm an evil bastard and there should be no doubt believing it.'

'Danny, come and eat.'

I felt tearful but didn't want to give in to it and so made my way to the food. If I was eating, then I was thinking about something other than the miserable day I'd had and using the muscles in my face and jaw and throat to stop the tears.

'Do you want me to sit with you?' I didn't. I wanted to be left alone but there'd been dozens of times when he'd been mad busy and dropped everything to sit and talk to me when the mood was on me. There were times when he'd stayed hours after his shift had ended to talk to me, to listen.

'Yeah, thanks, Tom, that'd be nice. Do you want the news on?'

'I thought you didn't watch the news!'

I didn't watch the news, ever, quite deliberately so, because you never knew what was coming next and it was just a horror show too far. Tom, however, was an addict.

'I might be on it.' I leaned over and ended the discussion by switching on the box. It was the BBC Six O'

Clock bulletin. I turned and cut open my lasagne. The news was nothing more than a noise in my ears and a band of colours at the edge of my eyes.

'*Danny!*' Tom's voice cut across the sensory blanket of sound and vision. 'Danny, look at the television!'

'Halloween,' I said, turning to look. In the top right-hand corner, the word **LIVE** remained constant as images of a motorway pile-up filled the backdrop to the reporter who spoke to camera.

There was darkness, and chaos, noise and wreckage being towed away, while ambulances arrived and departed and the police and fire crews worked around the paramedics.

The reporter peered into my eyes, and spoke softly, 'There are more than forty vehicles involved on the road leading to London and at least fifteen on the road to Oxford who've crashed because they lost concentration to what was going on on the other side. It's a vision of hell!'

I didn't want to watch any more, I wanted it to all go away. But I was freezing by the moment, turning to marble beneath my skin. The TV revealed a graveyard of mangled metal, shimmering in the slanting rain and the sodium lights above it all.

'Ambulance crews and fire engines from Essex and London have been drafted in to cope with the survivors . . .'

'It's him,' I said, softly.

'What, Danny?' asked Tom, his eyes still pinned to the screen.

'It's him.'

The reporter's mouth moved but I couldn't hear because my head was filled with the crazed music of a carousel.

For a moment, I was thrown back to the multi-screen cinema, near the place that used to be home, watching myself up on the big screen, standing in a deserted fairground, watching a carousel light up and come to life, turning by itself in the dead of night. It spun in slow motion and on the first horse was Richard Pike smiling and waving at me, calling, 'It's you, Daniel!' as he went past, followed by Parkinson, slumped across the horse's head, and Kyle hanging off side saddle, and Kathy in a hunting coat with her head smashed open, and the dead and the dying from the motorway on horse after horse after horse after horse. And then the moment was gone and the bloodly pictures inside my head went away.

'It's him!' The sound came back from the television, and a voice asked, 'What about rumours that a Force K security van was responsible for the accident?'

'David, eyewitnesses are claiming that it was a Force K security van at the head of the collision. I've seen the wreckage of the van, myself. There are reports that a remand prisoner being taken back to jail from a court appearance has escaped. It's being speculated that it's Richard Pike – the so-called Invisible Man – who's absconded. But the authorities won't confirm this.'

'It's him. It's definitely him! Halloween,' I said to Tom. 'The night all evil things walk the earth!'

29

Out There in the Great Big
Beautiful World

'It's been confirmed that during the pile-up on the M40 on Thursday night, Richard Pike escaped from a Force K security van.'

I now watched all the news broadcasts on TV and, in between, listened to the radio.

'Pike was returning to prison after the first day of his trial at Oxford Crown Court when the vehicle he was travelling in overturned resulting in a multiple collision.'

His face appeared on the screen, a police mugshot from the day we were arrested, his eyes empty, his face stone but there was a smile buried deep in his features.

'Police are warning the public not to approach this man as he is highly dangerous.'

The thought of him approaching people sent a coldness across my scalp that made me sure it had already happened.

We'll meet again . . . Don't know where, Don't know when . . . I could almost hear him singing down my ear, like he was sitting next to me in the room. I turned the TV volume up and his voice faded away. *But I know we'll meet again . . .* He was speaking to me in song. I was waking up in the night with the song in my head, imagining I could hear it in the interference on the radio, picking up the melody as the wind picked a fight with the trees. I had a constant headache.

Tom let me have his papers – *Daily Mirror* and the *Guardian* – which was good because it meant I could scour them after midnight when nothing was reported on the TV. I was looking for him, the violent touch of his hand, lurking in the newsprint and I had the feeling it wouldn't be long before I found him.

★　★　★

Four days after he'd escaped, on the Monday morning, shortly after half past nine, the trial was abandoned by Judge Warlock and the jury, some plainly disappointed, but most clearly relieved, were dismissed and allowed to go back to their normal lives.

Warlock looked angry, very angry indeed, when he told me, 'You're to remain in the care of the local authority until an alternative trial date can be fixed and this debacle sorted out.' He held a finger out at me, jab-jabbing it into the air, as if he wanted to poke my eyes out. 'Don't leave this court thinking that your co-accused's escape will help you any. It won't. It will just serve to lengthen your time in council care.' His anger grew as he gazed into the empty space beside me in the dock.

I tried not to smile and looked to the public gallery where Dad had his arm around Mum. She waved as they led me back down to the cells.

'I didn't think he could just jib the trial like that,' I said.

'They can do what they like,' Kerr replied.

'What a lucky break!' Jones nearly broke out into song. 'Richard's done you the biggest favour he could have done.'

We drank styrofoam cups of tea, the nearest to champagne we could find in the basement of the county court.

'So what happens now?' I asked.

'We wait and see. If he gets caught,' said Kerr, picking pieces from the rim of her cup.

'If? What do you mean, if?' I was puzzled.

'Do you know how many serious offenders, I mean rapists and murders included, have escaped in the past five years?'

'No idea.'

'Two thousand. And a hundred of them are still on the run. If he manages the first month, his chances of staying on the loose are good. The police'll more or less give up on him . . .'

'Why?'

'Because they've got new crimes to solve,' said Jones, 'and new criminals to chase. They haven't got the time, money or manpower. As far as they're concerned, they've done their job.'

'But that's terrible,' I said.

Kerr straightened as she stood up. 'Look on the bright side, Danny. Warlock was talking blue chip rhubarb back there. Pike's done you a world of good. Any shred of credibility he might have had's gone straight down the toilet and right round the bend.'

I felt a five-year-old's Christmas morning buzz. Maybe my luck was changing. It certainly felt that way.

★ ★ ★

The news came just after lunch time in a single paragraph at the bottom of page seven of the previous day's *Sunday Mirror*.

A 32-year-old woman is recovering in intensive care at St Mary's Hospital in Orpington, Kent, after being savagely attacked in her home on Halloween. Police are treating the case as attempted murder.

It was him. I had no logical reason to be sure of this but I had a cast iron hunch that made me certain this was his work.

I read it over and over until I could close my eyes and see the words in negative white letters printed against the dark canvas of my mind's eye, the words rumbling from my heart and passing over my lips like a mournful prayer. The words flashed on and off in my brain as if triggered by a fluorescent light; they crossed my eyes and ran round the span of my skull like they were on a never-ending loop as I sat on the floor chanting them into my fists.

And then I was silenced. My eyes opened and mouth closed as the sudden and breath-catching light of inspiration hit me. If he'd wanted to kill the woman, then there was no doubt in my mind that she'd have been dead.

Which made me wonder, if he hadn't wanted to kill her, then why did he attack her? Which begged the question, if he hadn't wanted to kill her, then what did he want? What was going on?

On TV, World War II veterans were getting ready for Remembrance Sunday, a coachload of old men, in their best suits, each wearing medals and ribbons and regimental berets. They were having a singsong. 'We'll meet again . . . Don't know where . . . Don't know when . . . But I know we'll meet again some sunny day . . .'

30

DNA

I insisted on seeing Parker and Waites, as I had information about Pike, and was surprised when Waites turned up with another detective who I'd never seen before. As he set about fixing up the tape, Kerr pointed at him and asked Waites, 'Who's this?'

'DC Stretch,' replied Waites. He was in the sort of foul mood that made mad dogs romp into the wilderness with fear in their hearts.

Waites wore check golf trousers, blue moccasins and a pink V-necked sweater and, I noticed, for all his dark expressions, he looked like a joke.

'So where is she?' I said.

'Austria,' he answered. 'She got a cancellation, after Warlock abandoned the trial. She's gone skiing.'

'What about you? Didn't you fancy getting away from it all?'

'I was on my way to play golf when I was called in to come and see you? It's the first chance to play I've had in four months.'

'Four months without golf?' I stated. 'I think you'll find the disruption to your game worth it.'

'I do hope so, Daniel!' This was the first real emotion I'd seen in him, anger. Murder clearly didn't get to him but ruined golf really hit the rage bull's-eye. I'd screwed up his day so, as winter sunshine splashed in through the window, I rubbed it in a bit further, 'It's a nice day for it too.'

Waites pressed record and as he went through the formalities of opening the interview, he mellowed the tone out in his voice.

'Daniel, you contacted us and told us you had some information about another serious crime, committed by Richard Pike.'

'Yes, I did.'

'So, what is it you want to tell us about?'

I handed him the *Sunday Mirror*, open at page seven and with the small article circled in blue biro. 'Read that!' I told him and he read it out loud in a neutral voice that could have come from a robot. He handed the paper back with a face to match the voice.

'So, what's your point, Daniel?'

'My point is, the attack you've just read about, was committed by Pike.'

'How do you know that?'

'I just do.'

'You were locked up here on the night of 31st October. Right?'

'Right.'

'So how can you say it was him? Have you been in touch with him?'

'No. How could I?'

'Or has he contacted you?'

'No. How could he?'

'Then what are you talking about?'

'I read this and had a gut feeling. It's him. I know it is. I know he did it.'

'Did he tell you, if I escape I'm going to Kent to attack a woman?'

'No.'

'Then what are you on about? Did you know he was planning to escape?'

'No, I had no idea. How could I?'

'But you know he committed this crime . . .'

'Yes.'

'How?'

'I've told you. I have an instinct about it.'

'Have you anything else you wish to say, Daniel?'

'Yes.'

'Go ahead!'

'How's the victim?' I needed to know. 'How's the lady he attacked.'

'She's . . . she's recovering very well. She's out of intensive care.'

'Has she been questioned yet?'

'Not yet. But she will be, as soon as possible.' Waites was clocking the sunshine outside. 'Anything else, Daniel?'

'I've said all I have to say!'

As Stretch tidied the tape machine away, Waites hovered near the door, a man plainly in two minds. His face grew dark as bongos went off in the back of his brain.

'Goodbye!' I called as he and Stretch left the room.

Waites looked around and threw a hand up for a fraction of a moment.

'Are you going to cough, or are you going to keep it to yourself?' I asked.

'Look, I know you can't have been in touch with him and I know he can't have been in touch with you, Daniel. And you were in no way involved with the escape. So, logically, this doesn't add up.' I waited quietly. 'Daniel . . . just off the record, are you psychic or something?'

'Why do you say that?'

'It'll be common knowledge soon.'

'What'll be common knowledge?'

'Kent Constabulary, they've got forensic evidence from the scene of the crime. She put a fight up and, she cut him. It *was* Pike who attacked her, his blood's all over the house and the DNA's definitely his. I'll pass the tape on to them. I'm sure they'll want to talk to you. They'll be in touch.'

Something happened in the sky, the clouds shifted suddenly because the sunshine in the room came razor sharp and ultra bright, and just as quickly faded.

'Any sightings of him?' I enquired. 'Any hint of him?' My heart was banging but I spoke slowly and quietly.

Waites laughed and shook his head. 'What do you think?'

31

Bonfire Night

When they threw Guy Fawkes onto the bonfire, arms of flame rose to the night sky chased by a cheer while the straw man ignited and collapsed into the red hot heart of the blaze. Tom told me that the effigy was a scarecrow given to the home by a neighbouring farmer.

I stood at the window, watching the fireworks and envied the people outside, the touch of the cold hand of the winter night and the warmth of the fire. I imagined the colours of the fireworks against my skin and the smell of cordite, the taste of charcoal on the food that came off the barbecue as fast as it was cooked.

I came away from the window and lay face down on the bed, my mind returning to the same old question that had bugged the skin off my teeth for a whole twenty-four hours. Why didn't he finish her off? Why did he allow her to live?

The escape had sunk from sight from the newspapers and TV bulletins but every day, brand new violent crimes were reported. The same hunch that told me he'd done the Orpington attack told me he hadn't done it again. And every passing day when he wasn't caught bolstered his chances of making his escape permanent, a thought that made me sit up straight on the bed, get to my feet and look into the shadows at the corners of the room.

I had a mental picture of him, standing in some dark place, lit up for a moment by headlights, smiling, then synthesising back into the darkness.

I turned on the TV to rub away at the edges of my loneliness and watched the BBC Ten O'Clock News which was just starting. No sign of him in the headlines so he was still out there. My scalp came alive, the nerves in my skin vibrated and the loud and sudden knock at my door made me gasp.

'Can I come in?' It was Tom. 'Get your jacket on, they've sent a car for you.'

'Who's sent a car for me?'

Stretch and a uniformed officer appeared in my doorway, jangling a pair of handcuffs. 'What's going on?' I asked.

'You're wanted, at the station,' said Stretch. 'Will you please put your jacket on quickly, we've got a car waiting downstairs.'

★ ★ ★

On the way there, they wouldn't speak with me and every *no, don't know,* and *couldn't tell you* made the darkness outside press down hard on the silence inside making me afraid and vulnerable and desperate.

'Please, will you just tell me if I'm in any more trouble?'

'I don't know!' yawned Stretch.

'Are you taking me to Kent?'

'I don't know.'

By the time we pulled into the parking area at the back of the station, I was convinced I was about to be slammed with every unsolved killing this side of my eleventh birthday, and as we got out and made the short walk inside, my terror was replaced by a jet black mood of resignation. Injustice? I should be used to it by now.

When we arrived, I couldn't believe the first thing I saw. I blinked and wondered if I was stuck in some surreal dream. Kerr was standing at a vending machine, drinking coffee and laughing with Waites.

Stretch uncuffed me and said, 'Wait here!' as he carried on and disappeared through a set of swing doors.

'Danny!'

She smiled, was about to speak but I got in before her with, 'Why am I here?'

She looked to Waites who was straightening up his tie and then buttoning the front of his jacket. 'There's been a major development,' said Waites. 'That's why you're here.'

'What development?'

Stretch returned, brandishing a set of keys and called out, 'Number 2's free!'

Waites held my arm and told me, 'Come on!'

'Why don't you save yourself the trouble of questioning me and just charge me with whatever it is you think I've done!' I pressed my body weight down on my heels and refused to move a step forward.

'Danny,' Kerr whispered. 'It's good news for a change. Let's go!'

★ ★ ★

231

'For the benefit of the tape recorder, I'm showing Daniel a copy of the audio cassette of an interview between DCI Fortuna of Kent Constabulary and Ms Joanne Marsden, the victim of attempted murder . . .

'And I'm now placing the cassette into a second machine that is on the desk between us.' He pressed *play* and said, 'Listen to this!'

I stared at the spools as they turned around and waited for the silence at the beginning of the tape to end. Then a woman's voice entered the interview room through the built-in speaker in the cassette recorder.

'Joanne, do you feel well enough to talk?'

There was a longish pause before she responded with a fractured and weak sounding, 'Yes.'

'Do you feel well enough to discuss what happened last Thursday?'

'Yes.'

'In your own time then, Joanne?'

'Can I have a drink of water?' She was weak, sick-sounding and injured, her voice strained with pain and echoing shock. My whole being was glued to the machine and the voices. Waites turned up the volume a little and I could hear her sipping from a glass, I could hear her clear her throat, the sound of the glass being placed down on a wooden surface.

'Last Thursday, Halloween . . .' she said, slowly. A picture of her flashed through my mind, propped up in a hospital bed, bruised and battered, hooked up to a drip. 'I was in the kitchen of my house . . . it was about seven o'clock at night . . . I was making a salad . . .'

'You live alone?'

'Yes. I'd been to the front door twice because of kids calling to trick or treat and I heard the bell go and thought, I won't answer. But the bell just rang on and on, so I went to the front door and called, "Take your finger off the bell!" But the bell just kept on ringing. I opened the door and there was no one there. I stepped out. The bell had been stuck down with a plaster, so I took it off. I looked around. Nothing. Then . . . a car went by and, just for a second, there he was standing in the path, picked out of the dark by the headlights.' She stopped talking and started crying. 'It was like he flew at me, literally flew at me, right into me, bundling me into the hallway before I had a chance even to scream, it was just so fast . . . I still had the salad knife in my hand. He kicked the front door shut and then he had his foot on my throat; I was on the floor, so I swiped at his leg with the knife and he . . . laughed. He took his foot off my throat. I ran to the kitchen to try and get out the back way but he followed me, laughing his head off! He got me at the kitchen door and I lunged at him with the knife and he grabbed hold of the blade with his hand, and pulled it away from me, he was smiling at me . . .'

She paused, took a drink. 'The blood was seeping out of his fist. He punched me in the face, hard, two or three times. He threw the knife down and grabbed a tea towel, wrapped his cut hand up, his leg was bleeding. I just curled up on the ground and he said, "*Get up, Joanne!*" . . . which made me think, *Do I know him?* I recognised him then, from his picture in the papers, the

Invisible Man. He lifted me up by the armpits and I started shaking and screaming and he banged my head against the kitchen door, five, six, seven, he counted out each time he banged my head and he looked bored to death. He looked like it was a chore. Eight, nine, I blacked out.

'When I woke up I was sitting at my dinner table, tied to the chair but sitting up . . .' A picture formed in my head, I could see a woman sitting at the table, tied to the chair and, as she supplied the details, the room around me seemed to fade away and I was transported to her house, watching what happened on Halloween. 'There were candles on the table and romantic music playing on the CD. He was sitting opposite me. I could see him smiling through the candlelight as I came round. My head was splitting with pain and I could taste blood in my mouth. He raised a glass of wine and said, "*Here's to us!*"

'I said, "Let me go, please let me go!"

'He laughed and said, "*Don't be absurd.*"

Don't be absurd . . . his voice filled my head . . . *Don't be absurd* . . . I could see him, and hear him speaking the words.

'He moved over and sat next to me . . .' I closed my eyes and my head was filled with the scene she described on tape, my imagination turning her words into vivid pictures.

Joanne carried on, 'He stood up, he stood up at the table and moved over to me. I was afraid, I was crying when he sat next to me. My hands were tied behind my back and tied to the back of the chair. He wiped the tears from my face and I said, "Please don't hurt me!" '

She was quiet for what seemed like a week.

' "*It's impossible to eat with your hands tied behind your back, Joanne, I know that, so I'm going to feed you.*" That's what he said to me.

'He'd finished off making the salad, there was a leg of chicken on the plate next to the lettuce and tomatoes and cucumber and spring onions. He cut a slice of cucumber into two semi-circles and raised them on the fork to my mouth saying, "*Open wide, Joanne!*" It was like chewing concrete but I tried to eat because I thought if I do what he says he won't kill me but I couldn't swallow the food, I just couldn't swallow. I baulked and threw up. He raised a glass of mineral water to my lips and ordered me to drink it. I took a sip. He picked the chicken leg from my plate and started eating it, ripping the flesh from the bone with his teeth, licking the pink bone and saying, "*Tasty, Joanne, very, very tasty!*" He offered me the other side of the chicken leg but I clamped my mouth shut and squirmed on the seat. "*Don't be like that, Joanne!*" He whispered to me, like he was my boy-friend and we were getting over a lovers' tiff. "Just let me go!" I begged him. But he shook his head and looked into my eyes, "*I've got something to tell you. You're going to die tonight, this is your last supper.*" He made it sound like he was offering me a kindness. I started weeping . . . out of control . . . and rocking the chair, straining against the knots on my legs and arms. He sat there as calm as the grave and drank more wine and finished off the chicken leg until . . . I just gave up and sat still, sobbing and trying to catch my breath. He sighed and blew his cheeks out and raised my chin with the chicken bone, so that I had to look into his eyes.

' "*Tonight's the night you die but before you go, I want to tell you something!*" He took my head in his hands, his bleeding palm wrapped in paper towels. "*Are you listening? I've been a naughty boy, Joanne. I killed a little boy and I killed a young woman and I . . . I made it look like someone else was responsible.*" He poured himself a large glass of wine and downed it in one gulp. "*This Daniel, I took his jacket and his knife and cut this little boy up because . . . I felt like killing him. I didn't want to get caught so I made it look like Daniel had done it. He was asleep in a hotel bedroom at the time. I even took his trainers to leave a footprint in the kid's back. Wasn't that cunning? Then I went and did it again. A young woman. Daniel was nowhere near at the time but I made sure the blood rubbed off on him. I told the police it was his idea. I wanted him to share my crimes. I knew he'd never take part in the killing, so it was the only way of involving him, in sharing the killing with him, in me and him being tarred by the same brush forever and ever. And, Joanne, I want you to take my secret to the grave.*" He stroked my face with the back of his hand. I could hardly breathe but I managed to say, "Why?"

' "*Why what, Joanne? Why do that to Daniel? Why do this to you? Because . . . you are my victim and I own you and he is my victim and I own him and some victims get to die and some victims get to live but you all get a share of one thing, you get to share in the pain, in my pain. Do you understand? I'm giving you a gift, I'm sharing with you, with Daniel, with Kyle, with . . . I can't remember her name. Poor Daniel. I had to tell someone about Daniel, and it was you. Does that make you feel privileged? Answer the question. Do you feel privileged to share my secret?"*

' "Yes. Let me go! I won't tell anyone your secret, you don't have to kill me."

' *"You're not listening, Joanne. Just accept that. Tonight, you're going to die!"*

' "Please . . ." I begged and begged him for mercy . . . and he said, *"Joanne, you're becoming a bore!"* He reached into his pocket and pulled out a stone about the size of a fist and raised it above my head . . . That was the last thing I saw, the stone in his fist coming down on my head . . .'

The room was filled with the sound of her crying, her anguish flooding from the tape machine. My eyes focused on the spools of the cassette turning round and round until Waites stopped the tape. There was a silence in the room, a silence so dense that it filled the lungs. I stared at the cassette because I didn't know where else to look. Miss Kerr laid a hand on my shoulder and offered me a crumpled paper handkerchief. I wiped the tears from my eyes and face and sat up straight.

'The Kent police got there just in time. She'd have died if they hadn't arrived on the scene when they did,' said Waites, basking in reflected glory.

'You reckon?' I retaliated. He frowned at the severe tone of my voice. 'How'd they know to go to her house?'

'Telephone tip-off from a suspicious neighbour.'

As he spoke, I saw the penny dropping in Waites' mind.

'Richard made that call,' I said.

'You understand what this means?' Waites looked at me. I knew but I stayed dead silent and gave no physical response. 'You're off the hook, Danny!'

Miss Kerr explained, 'With a confession like that under those circumstances, he's damned himself. He's validated everything you've said, all along.'

'You can't go tonight, there's some formalities we have to go through,' Waites said.

'But, Danny,' Kerr smiled broadly. 'It's wonderful. You're free!'

I leaned towards her and kissed her on the cheek. She wrapped her arms around me and my lips lingered near her ear. 'But only because he wants it like that, Miss Kerr,' I whispered. 'Only because he wants it.'

32

Epilogue
Two Months Later

He was out there somewhere but I'd have gambled a decade off the end of my life they weren't going to catch him. He probably looked and sounded like a different human being from the one I'd encountered.

Each new day was a step forward, each day my mind gave a little less room to him and the things that had been and gone. Each day, the time between thinking of him stretched a little further and the image of his face grew a little fuzzier, though his eyes and their blueness came at me from a hundred different places: flowers, fires, sea and sky.

Each day, I was winning back a little more of the thing I thought I'd lost forever. Normality. At night, I no longer had any memory of my dreams, only the dull sensation when I woke up at three in the morning that I'd forgotten something extremely important, something I could never put my finger on, something I'd never recall. Like a part of my mind was gone for good.

★ ★ ★

I was woken at seven each morning by the sound of the

letterbox snapping shut and the dull thud of mail on the mat.

One morning, three weeks after Christmas, I went downstairs to a small puddle of white envelopes and a brown jiffy bag with my name and address printed in thick black felt tip. The postmark was a complete blur of dark ink but the stamp on the package was English.

I made my way into the living room where I turned on the gas fire and sat on the floor, turning the jiffy bag over and over in my hands.

My fingers tingled as I realised the object inside, the hard, rectangular content, was a video tape. The clock on the video blinked on and off, inviting me to open the bag and play the tape. I don't know how long I sat there, feeling no benefit from the fire as the cold of morning spread inside me.

I found a small hole in the body of the bag and, tearing open the skin, sent a cloud of dust and fibre floating towards the ceiling. But as the dust was drawn to my nose, I thought I could detect his body scent.

The clock blinked on and off at me, 8:03, 8:03, as the mouth of the video gaped open to swallow the tape whole. There was nothing on the case, no word of a clue. My hand explored inside the envelope but there was nothing there, no note or message, nothing. I pressed *play* and turned the screen to a heaving mass of electronic silverfish which shifted to an image of cliffs. It was a row of white cliffs and a black sea churning and chopping and wild waves and white spray thrown up from the passage of a ship through the water. There was the throb of a ship's engine and seagulls, gulls which swept in and out of the picture. I recognised the cliffs – I'd stood and watched them loom up on the horizon when I'd come back from France. I'd watched them from more or less the same spot as the video was being taken. I had a very strong and particular memory of this thing and the video was like a recording of my memory. It was Dover, the English Channel, the ferry going back to England.

'Daniel, are you OK?' His voice skated over the image of cliffs and leaked out of the TV speaker like nerve gas. 'Recognise this place, Daniel? You should do! I'm standing on the same spot as you did, the summer before last. I can sense you. I can sense you've been here.'

The cliffs were getting larger as the ferry came nearer to the shores of England.

Richard Pike walked into the eyes of the camera, his face framed by the white cliffs and he smiled at me.

'Daniel, we've been apart for too long now. I've been away but I'm coming back. Please don't think I've forgotten you or abandoned you. I haven't. Really, I couldn't. You and me, until the end of time, us.'

I held the jiffy bag to my mouth and baulked. My entire being was in a spasm of agony as I was sick, sour and burning, as tears swam down my face. The waves crashed at the sides of the ferry and I could hear the blood pounding in my head.

'You didn't think I'd leave you, did you, Daniel? Or forget about you?'

There wasn't a trace of mockery in his voice, not a hint of laughter at my expense. His tone was warm and friendly and loving. His mouth opened and closed and his words flew at me like sugar-coated razor blades.

'We'll work everything out once we're together. I'm sorry about . . . the way things worked out last March. I'm sure you understand. I'll come for you and it'll be just like the good old days. You and me, Daniel, us.'

It started to rain onto the camcorder lens and he sang, 'We'll meet again, don't know where, don't know when but I know we'll meet again some sunny day!'

I could see the port, the ships and the future.

The image on the screen was fading to darkness. 'Daniel, I love you and I'm coming home. Wherever you are, wherever you go, I am with you . . . always!'

I rewound the video and watched it over again, pausing the tape, freezing *his* features, gazing into the darkness where his mouth opened to greet me, staring at each and every fragment of his face, the face that had lurked in the dark places of my mind for months and months. There was a point of light twisting out of the darkness in his eyes, a glimmer that illuminated their distinctive blue, the blue I'd seen wherever I'd looked since meeting him, the blue in the sky and the sea, the blue found in fire and flowers.

I rewound the video and watched it in slow motion, my face drawn close up to the screen, my eyes locked into the slow shifts and rhythmic blinks of his eyes. 'OK!' I said, my voice little more than a whisper.

I rose to my feet, my eyes locked into his on-screen gaze. *What was that he'd said?* I stopped the tape, rewound it, played it at normal speed and listened again.

'I'll come for you and it'll be just like the good old days. You and me, Daniel, us!'

'OK!' I replied, my voice stronger and louder, as he sang 'We'll Meet Again' to me. I hit the stop button and blacked him out of the room.

I drew back the curtains and threw open every window in the room, cold, clean air flooding into the house, warm, stale air and the echo of his voice drifting out.

I didn't hear her arrive and I didn't know how long she'd been there but Mum was in the doorway, her face networked with sheer anxiety. 'Danny, are you all right?'

'I will be,' I replied, as I walked up to her and kissed her. 'I will be,' as I walked past her and up to the front door.

'Where are you going?' she asked.

He knew where to find me, there could be no doubt of that.

I stepped out of the house as the first rain of the day fell and walked down to the gate, following a stray scrap of breeze-blown newspaper. I clasped the gate with both hands and, looking up and down our road, pressed the weight of my entire body into the ground on which I stood.

'Danny?' Mum spoke from the front door. 'Danny, come inside.'

'You go inside, Mum,' I answered.

'Danny, what are you doing, son?'

'I'm waiting.' My hands turned white as I grasped the gate tighter still.

'Waiting? Waiting for what?'

I kept my eyes fixed on the road that led to our house, the road that led to me.

'Danny?' Mum's voice was like a fading echo from a distant dream. 'What are you waiting for?' I didn't answer and after a minute's silence that seemed to last an hour, I heard her close the front door as she went back inside.

This time I was ready for him.

'I'm expecting a visitor.'